Filthy

ACQUISITIONS

EDMOND MANNING

Filthy ACQUISITIONS

EDMOND MANNING

WILDE CITY PRESS

WILDE CITY PRESS

www.wildecity.com

Filthy Acquisitions © 2014 Hank Edwards
Published in the US and Australia by Wilde City Press 2014

Published by Wilde City Press

ISBN: 978-1-925180-25-1

Cover Art © 2014 Wilde City Press

Dedication

To Anne Tenino, for breakfast.

Chapter One

As his rental car gently cruised through the three-block downtown, Keldon tried to notice things that would make the town unique to him, local flavor. He mildly hoped for quaint, but found nothing of the small-town charm he expected. Instead he saw a chain gas station, a sad-looking pizza parlor with dirty windows, two chubby kids sitting on a curb drinking from 7-Eleven Styrofoam cups, though he could not spot the 7-Eleven itself. The downtown businesses seemed normal enough, a sewing shop (misspelled with the pretentious and empty *shoppe*), a tax business, a doctor's office with beige blinds and—

It was normal. Very normal.

This was his third visit to Monroe, Wisconsin, and he could not reconcile how absolutely ordinary the downtown appeared compared to the strange, repulsive purpose of his visit. He wanted the town to appear vaguely menacing, maybe a sinister machine shop or frowning old people in rocking chairs in front of local businesses, so he could use the material for a later anecdote, something about how the character of the town matched the perverse transaction he headed toward. But the ordinary brick façades with cement ornamentation refused to cooperate. Downtown Monroe was quiet. Sleepy, even. He passed an empty garden space with cow-painted columns and a sign welcoming visitors to come and sit. The garden sat barren, too early in spring to contain actual plants or seedlings.

The thought flitted across his brain that even if he could turn this into an anecdote, with whom would he share it? Which friends would he call? None. He didn't have friends anymore. He had dropped them, or they had dropped him. He scolded himself for getting distracted from his true purpose in Monroe. Keldon Thurman intended to stay only long enough to make the acquisition and leave.

Breezing beyond downtown and into the residential streets, he had no problem finding his destination, having already visited the Turners twice previously. He pulled onto their average street lined with unremarkable two-story homes. the Turners' trees almost perfectly spaced as the evenly spaced trees across the street and down the block.

The green was gradually returning, he noted. Like birds that had flown south, green flocked to the late-April treetops, resting on small branches, ready to burst into song. The grass was not minty-fresh, exactly, not cheerful spring, but rather a deadish-brown with hints of life and occasional mint-green smatterings. Soon these lawns would reveal themselves to be not dead, only sleeping. But not yet. He was just glad he did not have to deal with boots or a snow-covered sidewalk, which would have impacted how he presented himself.

He wanted to look crisp.

The Turners were expecting him, so when he pulled into their driveway at their white aluminum and brick façade home, he wasn't surprised to see the front door swing open. The lawn was scattered with a few outdoor toys in various states of abandon. He had not seen the children on the previous two visits and suspected they had been whisked away, far from the delicate negotiations required in selling and purchasing art created by a serial killer.

Keldon noted this fact—the missing children—and figured he might be able to use that if necessary. Of course, he was only supposed to drop off the check and pick up the art. But he did not trust the Turners. Everything was negotiable. He decided to take his time and make them wait at the front door.

He turned off the engine and straightened his power-red tie while walking himself through various contingency plans—how the Turners might try to back out and how he might turn the situation to his advantage. Or everything might go smoothly. But the first three acquisitions with other art owners had not gone as expected, and he had no reason to expect the one with the Turners would either. These paintings brought out the worst in everyone, he'd discovered. Before the first acquisition he'd wondered, *Who wants to own a convicted serial killer's art? Who wants that?* Well, now he had an answer. Donna and Gerald Turner of Monroe, Wisconsin.

He finally extracted himself from the front seat and retrieved his briefcase from the back, pretending not to notice Mrs. Turner waiting inside the front door.

The Turners disgusted him, his wealthy patron disgusted him, everything about this work disgusted him, a low-simmering burn in the back of his mind. But the moment that disgust threatened to evolve into a strong opinion, he reminded himself he did not care, he could not afford to care. He did this for the money. Keldon understood being disgusted with oneself. The Turners had flattered a serial killer for two years of that murderer's prison sentence so he would give them his original art. So what? For the money he would make brokering all fifteen pieces of serial-killer art, Keldon's nebulous morality could ignore the disgust, or at least mutter to itself in the corner.

Keldon slammed the car door and walked toward Mrs. Turner, flashing her a grin. He hoped it came across as more sincere than he felt.

She did not return it.

He wasn't surprised. She had never smiled at him, never extended him that basic courtesy. She stood with her arms folded, her dirty gray hair pulled up behind her head and clipped with a plastic comb. The baggy wrinkles tracing the contour of her face suggested a history of pouting and negativity. He disapproved of her overly orange fake tan. He suppressed the desire to comment on it, even obliquely. He had enough self-awareness to know his distaste for her was influenced by her treatment of him. Everyone wanted to be liked. But she acted as though Keldon were the enemy instead of an envoy sent by a wealthy patron.

"We have a problem," she said.

Keldon was not surprised in the slightest.

"Oh dear," he said, affecting surprise and disappointment. "That's terrible. Let's discuss it."

She turned and walked through the front door, and he followed. Keldon didn't care what the problem was. It didn't matter. He felt confident he would leave with the acquisition. The outcome was not in question.

There it was, propped against a leather recliner, the king's throne in the living room.

The painting itself was nothing remarkable: a sloppy unicorn with a wavering silver and pink horn, pawing and prancing before a two-dimensional blue lake. Blob fairies hovered in the background like squashed bugs. Merrick preferred small canvases; it would definitely fit in Keldon's briefcase. The technique was not impressive, sloppy brush strokes and clumsy attempts at adding distinction. Actually, he reflected, the word *technique* did not apply at all. The finished product contained all the charm of a paint-by-numbers completed by an inattentive ten-year-old. In fact, it could easily hide in a thrift shop unnoticed, forever scorned by anyone who happened to see it dangling from a crooked hook behind a box of jigsaw puzzles in the back corner. Except for its distinction: painted by a mass murderer. Suddenly, the ugly unicorn painting had value.

"Here's the thing," Mrs. Turner announced as soon as she had been reunited with her greasy-haired husband and his pointed Brylcreem moustache. She looked at him for confirmation, and he glanced at Keldon with uneasy eyes. "We think it's worth a lot more than you're offering."

Keldon nodded, wanting to give the appearance of seriously considering her. "What makes you think so?"

"Well, some friends of ours said we might get more money if we had an auction for it online. Said other people besides your rich friend might want it. A lot of rich people might want it."

Keldon studied them, their living room, re-evaluating the assumptions he had made about them and their lifestyle. A PlayStation and its corresponding cartridges and equipment dominated one-quarter of the living room floor, a giant flat-screen television plastered a nearby wall. Plastic knickknacks and faded landscape prints attempted to transform the bleak room into something cheerful and homey. They failed. Keldon noticed the plastic basket of unwashed clothes sitting on the patterned couch and found it depressing. Dirty plates and a pizza box sat unacknowledged on the coffee table near him. Knowing he was coming, they hadn't even bothered to straighten up.

All these details he recounted, reminding himself to make assumptions and observations but to resist becoming too attached to them. Through assumptions, he might learn how to conduct himself. But through assumptions, he could also misstep, so he constantly re-examined what he thought he knew and how he thought he knew it.

They hadn't offered him a seat.

"May I?" He indicated the couch.

Donna Turner inclined her head in irritated agreement, though the idea clearly did not please her. From her reluctance, Keldon understood they had planned to explain their decision to renege and then ask him to leave. His taking a seat was a fly in their ointment, a prelude to greater conversation they did not wish to have.

He realized he would have to pry the painting from their fingers. If not literally, then metaphorically.

"Auction where?" Keldon tried to sound pleasant. "No real auction house will have you because the item for auction is so reprehensible."

"Someone will take it," Gerald Turner said, finally contributing. "If they think it will get good bids, they'll take it."

"No," Keldon said, "they won't. Not Christie's. Not Sotheby's. Not Bonhams or Fellows. Sure, this painting may create some cash for them, but more important than a cut on an ugly painting is their reputation. Nobody wants to be the auction house that cared so little for common decency that they were willing to profit extensively from a serial killer's unicorn fantasy painted from death row. They aren't *ghouls*."

The arrow found its mark, and Donna Turner recoiled slightly, enough for Keldon to decide this approach worked. She understood that he had implied *ghouls* to mean them as well. He assumed the Turners wanted more money but not the publicity, and that would help him prevail. Keldon wasn't proud of what he was willing to do, the things he would say to win this negotiation. But he wasn't hired to be polite. He was hired to acquire the painting. His bonus—his future—depended on winning *all* fifteen paintings on the list. This was only the fourth.

Keldon adjusted the knot of his tie. "Would you take your grandmother's antique clock to the same auction house that represented *serial-killer art*? No. You would not."

"There's always eBay," Donna said defiantly, jutting out her chin.

"Yes," Keldon said, doing his best to look agreeable. "That would work. Of course, it would take months. Maybe a year. You couldn't sell the painting for full value without a rigorous validation process. You'd have to ship the painting to a laboratory where they could confirm the paint style, the brush strokes, and so forth. Standard wait time is six months depending on their backlog. I'm only estimating."

"It's real," Donna said crossly. "He sent it from prison."

"Absolutely," Keldon said. "I don't doubt you one bit. However, if you're going to sell ugly, undistinguished art where its only value is proven authenticity, you must have it evaluated and validated by credible outside sources. With the artist dead, if they don't have any valid means of confirming Merrick painted this, it could take longer. The process is expensive, too, several thousands of dollars paid before you even know if they can confirm authenticity. So, hopefully your big eBay auction would recoup those costs. You *might*. But usually, the people with a horrible fascination for serial-killer art aren't flush with money."

"Except your client," Gerald said.

"Yes," Keldon said pleasantly. "Except my client."

He physically witnessed the Turners' resolve crumbling, but instead of feeling triumphant, he felt nothing but irritation at the inevitable decision they would make. Keldon knew how to close this deal but resented that he had to re-convince them to sell as he had on both of the previous visits. He sensed they were driven by immediate financial gain, and the thought popped into his head that *like recognizes like*. He felt revulsion, though he could not tell with whom—them, the artist, his employer, or himself for accepting this job.

He smiled politely and did his best to look affable. "Of course, the negative publicity from selling serial-killer art for the most profit will make you media targets. People will come out of the woodwork to hate on you. I mean, what kind of *monsters* seek profit from other parents' inconsolable, lifelong grief? Once the media understands you entertained a decent offer but it simply wasn't *enough money* to satisfy…"

Keldon felt his stomach flip. It was an awful thing to say to them. He knew it. He definitely hated himself.

Gerald Turner stood up. "That's enough. You should leave."

Keldon remained seated. "I should. But have you thought about your own kids? Hand over the painting to me today, and you'll have money immediately and perhaps be able to pay off that shiny TV in the corner. I suspect you need this money real quick, given the way you have showered me with questions about payment and how soon you could cash the check. I'm guessing you need that money right now. You sell this on eBay and not only will it take time and cost you money, but your kids will grow up under the shadow of parents who sought to cash in on seventeen *murdered* hitchhikers and other victims, too. It will haunt them. It will haunt you."

Donna said, "We'll sell it anonymously. Nobody will know."

"Donna," Keldon said in a patronizing tone, and he saw her displeasure at his familiarity. "*We* found you with very little effort. How long do you think it will take for the media to find you? The whole world will find out. And since the killer is dead, the outrage and disgust will naturally turn to those profiting from his artistic endeavors."

Keldon had no clue how difficult it had been to find the Turners. He had only been given a manila folder with the Turners' information and told, "Acquire it." But he hoped he had overtly threatened them enough. Instinctively, Keldon felt his client would have no problem releasing the Turners' information to the press.

Donna jabbed a finger in his direction. "Hey, I corresponded with that asshole for sixteen months in prison, pretending to be a fan, an admirer of his lunacy just to get one of those paintings, because I knew it would be worth something one day."

Keldon nodded. "Yes. And you were right. My client found you and offered you money."

"I want more." She snapped her mouth shut. "This ought to be worth something. I spent sixteen months—"

Keldon held up a hand to interrupt. "If you're trying to impress upon me that you sank to the lowest possible depths of depravity in whoring yourself to a serial killer, don't worry, I believe you. I have no doubt you were vile in your letters. Trust me, *I believe you*. Why don't you sell those on eBay instead?"

She glared at Keldon, but said nothing.

"I wonder"—Keldon paused and gazed at the ceiling— "what you wrote to gain his favor. To make your letters really stand out. You probably pretended to be a teenage girl, maybe in the age range he liked to kill, and convinced him he was just *misunderstood*. If you two had only met some rainy night when you were walking home and become friends…yes, I'm sure the letters are something you'd be proud to show your kids. Your family."

"She earned it," Gerald said, his irritation growing to match hers.

"I'm sure she did," Keldon said. "So show the whole world. Publish the letters. Show them what small-town America can do when motivated by greed with no regard to decency."

They said nothing to Keldon but did not look at each other, either.

He feared he pushed too hard. He didn't know what she wrote, but her slight facial twitch suggested he wasn't far off the mark. Whatever she wrote, she didn't want it seen. Keldon didn't like the hard edge he now displayed, crisp and adversarial. He had said horrible things to the Turners. But they had agreed to the offer and since then had changed their minds, tried to renege. It was his job to see they followed through.

Keldon studied them both. "My client offered you a reasonable amount for the painting. I'd suggest you take the deal."

Donna Turner sputtered. "Your shitty client is no better than us. You can't show up here and act better than us."

"Yeah," her husband said, "he wants it too. Probably to sell online."

"Perhaps," Keldon said. "I have no idea why my client wants it. Today, I came with your check. I will hand it over after you sign the paperwork guaranteeing a full year's silence on this purchase. The gag order prohibits you from speaking to anyone about this transaction, relatives, friends, media—"

"We know," Donna said. "It's not fair. We should be able to talk about it."

"You may. In one year. As we discussed on my last visit, if you speak to anyone before the year expires, legally you owe my client one hundred thousand dollars. And since the only possession of yours with that value is your home, you'd be making yourselves homeless for the privilege of breaking the gag order. And I should probably impress upon you that my client has no problem pursuing the financial restitution of your home. He may not need money, but he will gladly see you punished. He's not the forgiving type. And if you think you can anonymously leak your news to a media outlet, remember that my client has the money to pay for investigators to track down a leak."

Donna said, "Tell Mr. Mercer to give us an extra $10,000. It's worth that much."

Keldon said, "No."

"You're not the boss," Gerald Turner said. "You shouldn't answer without your boss."

"Mr. Mercer will say no."

Donna crossed her arms. "We're not signing your piece of paper or turning over that unicorn shit until you take that offer to your boss and get it approved. You'll have to come back another day."

Keldon studied them. He thought about pushing the "what about your kids" angle again, but while they flinched with the perception of bad parenting, they didn't bite enough to convince him that was their greatest concern. They seemed a little too self-centered for that. It had worked with Acquisition Number Two, a bland painting depicting a sunrise over Saturn, but he did not believe that strategy would work again with the Turners.

Still, he felt they were close to caving.

"Okay," Keldon said. "I'll ask."

Keldon had established with his employer that today he would pick up Number Four. She had promised to remain on standby, so he texted his client. Mrs. Maggiarra had insisted Keldon present a fictitious art patron named Byron Mercer as the collector behind the acquisitions, so nobody would suspect her true identity. She pretended to be Mr. Mercer's secretary. Keldon typed while they watched.

Mr. Mercer, the Turners want an additional 10K. Also, Donna Turner probably defrauded Merrick in prison by misrepresenting herself. If that's so, the Turners may not legally have rights to the painting. Withdraw offer?

Keldon smiled pleasantly while they scowled. He knew he wouldn't wait long, and in fact, the reply came almost right away.

Disgusting. Drop the offer by 1K and give them four minutes to decide. If they decline, leave and call the police.

Keldon read the text and smiled. "Mr. Mercer counter offered."

He rose from the couch to stand before them, showing them the text exchange on his phone.

Within five minutes, he left the Turner home with the unicorn painting in his briefcase. He was glad to leave. He drove through town, past the garden with cow-painted columns, but when he passed the downtown Sewing Shoppe, he could not contain it any longer. He eased into a diagonal parking slot away from other cars, and after turning off the car, Keldon cried into his hands, sobbing for a full five minutes, but he did not know why.

Chapter Two

Cruising slowly through the remaining streets in Monroe, Wisconsin, Keldon wiped his eyes and reminded himself why he'd accepted the position collecting serial-killer art for a wealthy patron. Money. Lots of money. In fact, enough money to pay for him to attend a four-year university if that's what he wanted. All he had to do was successfully acquire fifteen paintings created by executed serial killer James Wayne Merrick. But to collect the full amount, Keldon was required to obtain every single one. No exceptions. All acquired through legal channels. That was an important clause in his contract—everything had to be done legally.

The money was essential.

Keldon had no money, no other prospects, no college degree, and no particular talents that he could employ for a livelihood.

Over and over, he had debated trading his good looks for his livelihood. He could escort. He was attractive enough. He rigorously maintained a physique that, while not bulging with chunky bodybuilder muscles, remained chiseled, and he prided himself on a classic V-waist necessary for visually pleasing aesthetics. Two years ago, Keldon had tried escorting a few times and found the idea and reality that others owned him, even if only for an hour, depressed him. One man had paid a substantial bonus to vilify him, calling him a "dirty whore" and "filthy piece of ass." Keldon had not known at the time how much that would upset him, how those words would follow him for weeks and months, chasing him down when he tried to make purchases with the earned money, or how the words would whisper and curl around him when he appraised himself in the mirror. Keldon didn't want to escort again. He had only done it out of sheer desperation.

However, in more honest reflections, he knew that he really had been an escort for the first half of his twenties, allowing himself to be kept by generous older patrons while he halfheartedly pursued a college degree. Art history classes seemed absurd when Steven decided to fly him to Italy to see historic treasures first hand. Research papers diminished in importance while entertaining Steven and then, a few years later, Aamir. In his more forgiving moments, Keldon might even define his relationships with both men as positive, loving experiences. But by the age of twenty-seven, the quality they craved—youth—had transferred to younger, greener pastures. Keldon found himself without a degree, without a patron, without skills. He owned an extensive wardrobe and had once possessed some valuable jewelry and trinkets, gradually sold to pay rent.

As he raced by corn field after corn field, eager to shed Wisconsin for Illinois' familiarity, he contemplated his employer, Catherine Maggiarra, the very real art patron behind the façade of Byron Mercer. She'd interviewed him. Explained her offer. Hired him on the spot, with a few conditions. Complete anonymity. He could tell no one about this job and his undertaking. She explained it would be a difficult secret to keep, but he barely heard a word she said. The incredible number of dollars waltzed through his imagination, paying off credit cards, staving off eviction for several years, getting in good graces with his landlord. He was tired of offering up unbelievable promises just as much as his landlord wearied of hearing them. Keldon had used up any lingering goodwill. If he were late one more time, the landlord promised to begin the eviction process.

When Keldon finally calmed himself to listen to the terms of her offer again, he confirmed he could handle the secrecy. No problem. He did not volunteer to her that he had no one in his life to tell. His parents had disowned him. Siblings did not dare contact him. His ex-lover, Steven, wanted nothing to do with him, no longer interested in fawning and impressing Keldon with trips and luxuries. Aamir? Keldon hadn't heard from him after being stood up at the airport. Nobody wanted Keldon around. He had no one to discuss his non-secrets, so what would a secret matter?

She'd also insisted Keldon not ask any questions about her mission, her reasons, or the need for the imaginary Mr. Mercer. Keldon accepted this readily as well. For the unimaginable sum she offered, he would have agreed to anything.

But who was she? Why was she so fascinated with art from a serial killer? Keldon couldn't understand. After the first few successes, when she'd confirmed he had not taken illegal action in any way, she had nodded, a tight business nod, a signal to the end of conversation. When he presented her the paintings, her face did not light up with satisfaction nor the sickly pleasure of greed and ownership. Keldon knew how to read people, how to gauge their reactions to better understand what they wanted and whether they wanted more. He did not like to think of himself as an escort, but he could not deny that he had honed his ability to interpret faces and desires as a practical skill to keep him in relationships with his older men. Still, he couldn't read her. He couldn't understand what pleased her.

As he considered what strange fate had brought him into her orbit, he kept circling one question. Why did she choose Keldon?

His outburst outside the Sewing Shoppe in downtown Monroe, Wisconsin, embarrassed him. He didn't understand why he had cried. Why had the encounter impacted him in that way? The last thing he remembered feeling as he'd left the Turner household was being bored, completely bored by the exchange. How predictable the Turners were asking for more money. How glad and relieved he felt to leave their angry mutterings behind.

Did Mrs. Maggiarra know he would react that way? Could she have predicted his inexplicable outburst, and was it related to why she'd chosen him? What if she eventually discovered his moment of weakness—would she fire him? There was no way she'd ever find out he cried. Never. But in his imagination, he couldn't stop seeing her appraise him in a new, disgruntled light. He hadn't even applied for the job—Mrs. Maggiarra had contacted him and requested he interview for this position. But why him?

When he saw the sign welcoming him to Illinois, he shuddered with relief. Though the state-line distinction was political and arbitrary, he felt safer, more connected with Illinois and the Chicagoland area. He did not like the loneliness of the corn, the wide open spaces. He felt lost without tall buildings and concrete under his feet, his connection to hurried civilization.

Keldon did not like crying and had successfully commanded himself not to do so on more than one occasion, so the outburst in Monroe bothered him more and more. He decided to ask Mrs. Maggiarra why she'd hired him. She might reveal insights that would help him understand why he had cried. Was the serial-killer connection more upsetting to him than he realized? He was only an hour and a half away from sitting in her study, an hour and a half away from presenting her with the fourth victory. He was glad the creepy painting was locked in his briefcase. Four acquisitions meant only eleven remaining before the unimaginable monies were his to command.

He tried to fantasize spending the money on rich wardrobes and wild nights drinking, buying bar drinks for others, but the previous year and a half spent in poverty taught him money was not fun, but a sacred commodity to be fearfully worshipped. He would not squander it buying strangers drinks. He would not buy new clothes or even purchase back his Rolex. He couldn't indulge foolish whims, even with this windfall. He understood poverty far too well. He could almost taste homelessness.

He had worked retail but was not good at it; worked as an administrative aid for six months and hated it. He couldn't type fast enough. He wasn't skilled enough on the computer. Most recently, Keldon had worked temp jobs and hated those too. He'd felt out of options, when suddenly the mysterious job offer fell into his lap.

* * * *

After he turned off the car in front of her home in Chicago's western suburb of Glen Ellyn, his questions regarding her strange mission renewed themselves. She lived on a street indistinguishable from the Turners' in a quiet, middle-class home with beige aluminium siding and green trim. No toys scattered her front lawn, just meager bunches of annuals and perennials. He did not recognize flowers by name, but he could tell they were cared for, grouped by color and size, ornamental grasses and shrubs creating an early summer on this lawn. It dawned on him that it was too early for all these flowers—late April. Who planted flowers before May? Though snow seemed unlikely, it was too early to have your lawn so rich with color. But what did she care? She was a millionaire, and maybe she liked to garden. The house itself remained distinctly middle-class, no better or more attractive than its neighbors shouldering either side. He had a hard time reconciling her money with this bland setting.

He stood on the front porch and touched the doorbell, which announced his arrival with matronly chimes.

A rayon butterfly flag fluttered to the right of the front door, faded enough that Keldon assumed it wasn't new. Keldon reviewed the assumptions he'd made about Catherine Maggiarra. She possessed upper-class money but middle-class tastes. He tried to imagine her lugging heavy bags of outdoor potting soil to the front yard but could not. He had never seen her relaxed or out of a business casual suit.

She was secretive and well-versed in legalese. The contract he'd signed was carefully constructed. He would have signed it under almost any circumstances, but she afforded him a generous stipend to hire his own lawyer to review it before signing. The lawyer was as bewildered as Keldon by the anonymity clauses combined with his promise to never ask questions, but to the lawyer, everything seemed legitimate: six figures for acquiring fifteen paintings. Of course, the contract never explicitly mentioned the artist by name, so the lawyer only knew the condition to fulfill the contract. Mrs.

Maggiarra was very thorough in her desire for secrecy. Keldon would have signed the contract with just about any conditions.

Catherine Maggiarra answered the door, staring at him expectantly.

She looked the same as when he had seen her last. Her thick gray hair fell in frizzy tangles, almost a wide triangle behind her shoulders. He suspected she did little to tame it. Today she wore an orange blouse, nothing remarkable other than its cheery color and silky sheen. Her face wore the creases and sags of a woman in her mid-seventies, which was the closest he could pinpoint her age. She might even be eighty, but if she was, she looked good. Her skin was not smooth or perfected the way rich elderly widows enjoyed, blemishes removed and flesh bumps made smooth with plastic surgery. She was not hideous; she wasn't covered in warts. But he couldn't help but notice her scattered liver spots or the flesh bump on her right shoulder at the collar of the blouse. Her expression was guarded, as it always was with him.

Keldon lifted the briefcase. "I have it."

"Good." She turned away from him, leaving the door open.

He followed her into the home and again stole glances in every direction, searching for some hint as to why she wanted these paintings so desperately. Her own art was ordinary: flowers in vases, a historical pastoral scene. The interior decorations were tasteful, bordering on simple, and he found that he liked her long, elegant taupe draperies, swishing in modest movements when the occasional April breeze invited itself in.

He followed her to the oaky den.

She was not fat, nor was she thin. She did not walk with the poise of wealth, nor did she drag herself through the house like an overburdened cleaning woman. She walked straight and tall, poised but self-conscious, as someone does when they are being followed. He glanced at the throw pillows on her fluffy white couch and the ornamental sconce against the lemon-chiffon wall. Everything was ordinary and suburban except for the mission she'd assigned him.

He sat in his designated chair without being told. She sat behind the desk and donned the gold-rimmed glasses she often wore when they discussed business.

"The fifth piece might be a little tricky," she said and opened a manila folder on her desktop. "My information shows the owner potentially does not know what she owns. We're not sure."

Keldon desperately wanted to know whom the *we* referenced, but one of her legal conditions was he could never ask questions unless they related to his own role in her operation. He understood others worked for her, others who gathered intelligence about who owned the serial-killer paintings and any unique challenges in acquiring them.

"I'd like to ask a question." Keldon watched her reaction.

She looked at him without approving or disapproving and waited.

"How is it possible the owner doesn't know she owns a painting by a serial killer?"

Mrs. Maggiarra did not need to reference her notes. "The painting was a gift from Carolyn Woullet to her sister, Irene. Carolyn Woullet is now dead. We do not know what communication passed between the two sisters, but we know that the surviving sister doesn't realize it's a James Wayne Merrick. We're fairly sure of that because Carolyn Woullet did not know it was a Merrick."

How could she be so sure of this information? It bothered Keldon that he would never know the answer.

She studied Keldon as he studied her.

She said, "Merrick gifted the painting to one of the flatterers who wrote to him in prison. The purchaser thought owning serial-killer art would be intriguing, but he later grew to believe the painting was bad luck, so he offered it at a garage sale without revealing the painter's identity. It looks as crappy as all of Merrick's other paintings, so god only knows why Carolyn Woullet bought it. But she did. She was a neighbor on the block, and the seller felt a little bad for not revealing who painted it. He asked about it once, a year later, how she was enjoying it. Carolyn explained she'd mailed it to her sister. That's how we know where it is now."

"Okay." Keldon knew he was not to ask follow-up questions, so there was little he could do but listen.

Keldon frowned. How could Catherine know so much about the two sisters' relationship? How could she have such incredible insider data and still need Keldon for the actual acquisition?

"How am I supposed to get the painting from this person if she doesn't even know it was painted by Merrick?"

"I've given this some thought," Mrs. Maggiarra said. "I'll set up the visit, like the others, pretending to be Byron Mercer's assistant. I'll tell her that we want to examine the art in her home, and if it's acceptable, we will buy all of it. The entire household of art. We'll never have to tell her which painting we truly want. Throw the rest away. Or more likely, after I have all fifteen paintings, I can return the rest of her art to her."

"Buy an entire household of art?" Keldon asked. "Doesn't that seem extravagant? Not to mention suspicious. Who would do that?"

She did not smile at him, not a trace as she said, "An eccentric millionaire named Byron Mercer. Irene Woullet won't care. She'll take the money."

"For a household full of someone's favorite art, you're going to have to offer her a lot more than you have the others."

Mrs. Maggiarra extracted a page and closed the file. "No problem. I've written a letter of intent for you to deliver. It's a generous offer."

The logic made no sense to Keldon. She refused to give the Turners additional money, but was willing to pay exponentially more for a household of art she did not want so she could acquire the one piece she secretly craved. Instead of revealing her true desire and negotiating for that piece, she would overpay immensely. It made his head spin.

She added a Post-it note to the front of the file and scribbled on it before handing it to him. "Irene Woullet needs the money.

She's terminally ill. She's roughly 600K in debt right now. Even if she never intends to pay off those bills, she could use the money for everyday expenses until she dies. Trust me. She'll take the offer."

He took the file from her fingers and noticed her simple gold wedding ring, the empty space around. Age was already transforming hers into an old person's bony fingers. Keldon found he could forget she was old. Her confidence struck him as somehow virile. He had met older gentlemen who possessed that confidence, not arrogance, a certain self-assured quality that what he desired would soon be his. She possessed a grace that was not masculine, but Keldon didn't know a word that expressed feminine virility, so he let the idea drop.

Keldon thought about his bizarre cry in Monroe and wanted to know why she'd hired him, if she saw something in him, weakness or otherwise, that would explain his breakdown. In her formidable presence, Keldon was less sure he wanted to know her answer, but he felt the overwhelming urge to ask, to understand. He commanded himself to remain calm and betray nothing.

"Why did you hire me?" he asked. "Why did you contact me?"

Her eyes narrowed, and she leaned back in her chair.

"I'm not asking about why you're collecting this art. I am not asking about your other employees or where this investigation stuff comes from. None of the topics you outlined. I just want to know why you hired *me*. Why you thought I'd be qualified for this."

She said nothing.

Desperate for some continuation of this conversation, he said, "I don't even know anything about art."

"Neither did Merrick." Mrs. Maggiarra got quiet again.

Keldon remained silent, waiting for her dismissal or answer, whichever came first.

"You came recommended." She watched him closely. "I put out a few feelers with people I trusted. I specifically asked for someone who could get their way. Someone who gets what they want, time and time again. A friend of a friend got back to me with your name."

Keldon felt her answer like a punch to his stomach but chuckled to hide his discomfort. "That's hardly a compliment."

"No," she said without smiling, "it wasn't. The person who recommended you said you were a man who always got what he wanted. It was definitely not a compliment. I don't know how he knew you, but I suspected he may have been an ex-lover or friend of an ex-lover."

Keldon said nothing but felt an overwhelming sadness that this was how he was known. He doubted Mrs. Maggiarra knew either Aamir or Steven, his only real boyfriends. Didn't seem likely. But she obviously knew someone who had observed Keldon with one of them. That made him feel worse, but he resolved not to think about it until later.

She continued. "I had my private investigator research you. Temp jobs. Heavy credit card debt. But you had the look I wanted, elegant, sophisticated, young. You're handsome, Keldon, which I suspect you use to your advantage. Your face is not delicate, exactly, but your bone structure is crisp and clean. Expensive, dark hair, gently curling behind your ears, mysterious, brown eyes. You were an art history major before you quit college, which somehow perfectly fits your distinguished looks. You can chat up anyone who has something you want, and without meaning to, you create distance between yourself and others that they perceive as haughty. Men of your good looks and sophistication make people nervous. You're the perfect emissary. I suspect that in your negotiation, the Turners were nervous asking for more money. Discussing money probably feels tacky around you, as if you're above the sordid topic of coin. They don't understand how much it motivates you."

"Ow," Keldon said. "Don't hold back."

She did not smile but shrugged slightly. "You asked. Before my retirement, I worked in Human Resources for a large company. I know how to hire. I know what to look for. You're hungry, cultured, and insistent. Perfect for this work."

Keldon wanted to prolong the conversation, though he reeled from her insights. Some struck him as accurate and others not as much, but he could not discern which ones were true.

"You had me investigated?"

"Don't worry." She dropped her gaze and shifting her attention to paperwork on her desk. "We found nothing of interest. Just your finances."

Keldon nodded to accept this. The words *nothing of interest* lingered. He believed it to be true. There was little of interest about him.

"Who recommended me?"

"I won't answer that. And I don't like questions," she said with finality. "I'd like you to go to Madison as soon as possible for Acquisition Number Five. Tomorrow. And I have two checks for you, your wages and a separate one for expenses. Like last time."

"Thank you. Do you have an interview set up with Number Five?" he asked.

Keldon wanted to gloss over the immense relief and giddiness he felt in having a healthy paycheck in his hands. He didn't want to betray how much it meant to him. Which seemed pointless, he reflected, as she'd just gotten through telling him that's why she hired him.

"Not yet, but I will call Irene Woullet in an hour, and unless she has a doctor appointment, I am sure she'll accept a meeting. I'll call you to confirm it."

She leaned forward. "Now, let's have it."

The interview was over, so Keldon silently accepted the checks she offered and handed over the unicorn painting.

Mrs. Maggiarra studied the unicorn, and without any affect, she said, "This is it."

She leaned it against a potted plant near her feet and walked Keldon to the front door.

As he stepped onto the front porch, Keldon found himself irritated by his ban on question-asking. "Why did you plant your summer flowers in April? Isn't it a little early?"

"I'm old. I can do as I please," she said. "I see no reason to wait."

She closed the door behind him with a solid thunk.

Chapter Three

Keldon parked the car across the street from his destination and tried to make assumptions and guesses about what he saw. The tea-colored mansion was only two blocks away, a block and a half, really, from Madison's Lake Monona. He liked the exterior color, creamy beige, and its darker trim and burnt sienna roof tiles. Although some might call this study in brown *boring*, he found the rich warmth perfectly suited the environment, letting the blue and silver sparkles from the cold lake and the yard full of rich evergreens showcase the stunning neighborhood to advantage. Even the pale blue sky with airplane trails seemed to frame the rich brown house, promising coziness inside, possibly cocoa.

He liked the assumption that cocoa was served inside. Although Keldon was no architect, anyone could see that a plump round turret like a castle tower, and interesting angles and shapes everywhere else meant the home was expensive. Very expensive. Glancing up and down the street, he recognized it was an expensive neighborhood.

A spring wreath with simple yellow flowers hung against a solid wooden door.

The gold knocker appeared polished, and he decided his assumption was correct. Money. Even if Mrs. Woullet were in debt now, she had once been rich.

Therefore, he assumed money would work here. They would not need much additional persuasion. They would need to be flattered with money.

Keldon felt a blush of surprise when a young man opened the front door, if not young, exactly, then definitely around his own age. Maybe thirty. He stood slightly taller than Keldon but close enough in height to look eye to eye. His dull eyes were dead, blank. In a split second, Keldon decided the man meeting his gaze was not a smart man. *Too bad*, Keldon thought. *He's cute.* The man was unshaven and looked as though he woke up ten minutes ago. His unkempt hair and scraggly half beard confirmed the impression of a man who didn't care about, or wasn't aware of, his own appearance.

"I'm here for Mrs. Irene Woullet." Keldon dragged out his big smile.

"Yeah," the man said. "She's here."

The man did not move from the doorway, just stared with his blank expression.

Keldon noticed the scrubs.

"You expecting someone?" the man yelled over his shoulder without breaking eye contact. "Visitor?"

A voice called back, "Let him in, Joshua, for Heaven's sakes."

The man appraised Keldon again and shrugged slightly, as if saying, "Why fight it?" He stepped aside and yet not out of the way, forcing Keldon to brush up against him as he passed through the front door.

"She's in there," the man said.

Keldon stomped his feet on the entryway rug, out of courtesy more than necessity, and walked across the polished oak floor toward a sitting room he assumed was the source of the woman's voice. He first noticed her wheelchair, hands folded across her lap. The word *proper* registered in him immediately, and Keldon understood why. She was younger than Keldon expected, maybe late fifties or early sixties, and projected the appearance of a librarian. She wore tasteful pearls and a modest gray blouse.

A knit afghan, muted colors of grape and burgundy, stretched across her lap and dangled on either side, not sloppily, but carefully arranged. Her graying blonde hair touched the top of her shoulders and had a gentle bounce to it. She was a woman who took care of her appearance, he could see that. She even wore a hint of dark lipstick, which somehow touched him. Maybe she'd dressed up for him, the visitor with the strange offer.

"I'm Keldon Thurman. I believe Mr. Mercer's assistant scheduled my visit."

"She did," said the woman, offering her hand. "I'm Irene Woullet."

Keldon crossed the few feet to take it. Her hand was warm, and he realized he had expected it cold and lifeless. Her grip was weak, almost nonexistent, and he was careful not to overshake.

The man in scrubs appeared in Keldon's peripheral vision.

"This," she said with a hint of disdain, "is Joshua. He's the nurse my daughter hired to watch me and make sure I don't set myself on fire."

The nurse grunted.

A flicker of something passed over Mrs. Woullet's face, something like dismissal or judgment, and Keldon took his cue from the woman he wanted to impress. While he murmured a polite hello to Joshua, he adopted a tone of aloofness.

"I like your suit," the male nurse blurted out. "I like your blue shirt."

"Thank you," Keldon said stiffly.

"Joshua," Irene said. "Take us to the library."

Moments later, Keldon was surprised to discover she really did mean a true library, situated toward the back of the first floor with built-in wooden bookcases lining all four walls, crammed so full of books that even a hundred shelves could not contain the massive collection. Stacks appeared to grow from the corners like fungus. The open books scattered around the room, on tables, on the back of a couch, and atop precariously balanced piles almost suggested a third-grade class had hastily vacated the room, leaving behind the extensive mess. Thick ferns poised on columns served as pleasant sentries around the room, meant to soften the severe appearance of books, books, and more books. Mrs. Woullet did not explain to her nurse how to navigate her through the room. He seemed quite familiar with the challenge and positioned her between a gap in books and furniture, seemingly perfectly tailored for her chair.

Keldon lowered himself into the brown leather chair across from her and tried to sit with extra poise, extra dignity in these auspicious surroundings. He tried not to be too impressed, but this library suggested heavy use, which did leave a favorable impression he could not deny. In the past two years, Keldon had developed a fondness for books as they represented free entertainment from the library. Upon a second and third glance around the room, he noticed a number of paperbacks, which seemed incongruous in this rich environment.

She invited Joshua to leave them, prepare tea, and he obeyed her silently.

Keldon politely asked about the room, the light coming from the south windows, and he asked about the thick eggplant curtains used to keep that light at bay. After a few minutes of general conversation, she broached the topic of his visit.

"It's unusual," she said delicately. "Someone phones you and wishes to buy every piece of art in your home. I honestly do not know what to think of this. Can you explain?"

Keldon shook his head. "I cannot. My employer possesses unusual tastes. Perhaps he saw something here at a dinner party years ago. Perhaps he saw a painting in a photo a friend of yours shared on Facebook. I cannot say. He does not take me into his confidence. He asks me to execute his wishes, and I do."

"It's been many years since my husband or I entertained," Irene said, smiling, and Keldon sensed he was being carefully studied. He wrapped himself with an empty smile so she would find nothing but charm.

She said, "My husband frequently hosted parties here for lawyers in his firm and high-profile clients. I never knew half the people. But I don't remember a Mr. Mercer. I would suspect this setup was a pretext for robbery, but I checked out Mr. Mercer's references and presence online. He's a rich, eccentric art collector. Mostly Asian-influenced sculpture. I don't actually own any Asian-influenced sculpture."

Keldon nodded and did his best not to react. He'd had no idea Mr. Mercer was anything more than a lie invited by Catherine Maggiarra. Clearly, Catherine had planned this deception much further than he understood. He'd never considered a man named Mr. Mercer actually existed.

"He's definitely eccentric," Keldon said.

The conversation continued along those speculative lines for a moment, Keldon doing his best to be polite and blank until Irene called for Joshua and he appeared on cue very quickly. Keldon imagined he was used to being summoned.

"Joshua, where is the tea?"

"I forgot to turn it on. I got distracted."

Keldon decided it was too bad Joshua's eyes seemed dull as the rest of him was quite handsome. He had thick muscled arms constrained by the scrubs, and a sexy heft to his weight. He was a man who perhaps worked out regularly, and his clumsy gait suggested he didn't quite understand how to balance the muscles he had built.

"Well, we may as well go tour the house art," she said gruffly.

With Joshua pushing her, Irene narrated the history of pieces, and Keldon asked questions, pretending he cared. He found himself behind Joshua as they walked room to room, appreciating the rise and fall of each ass cheek beneath Joshua's scrubs. The thin fabric caught in the deep cleft once or twice, and Keldon felt himself hypnotized by the beautiful curves he followed.

The remainder of the first floor gave the same impression as the library, mildly intimidating but somehow just this side of comfortable. The rooms were airy and large, furniture expensive and lush, but also draped with personal touches that did not exactly match high fashion. A ladybug needlepoint pillow rested against a robin's egg blue chaise lounge. A stained-glass lamp on a wrought iron stand suggested great artistry, but upon closer inspection, Keldon could see the stand was a gorilla posing in a slutty ass-thrust-out position. Like the paperback novels throughout the exquisitely wooded library, the second glance in every room revealed touches of ill-fitting glamour, whimsy in some cases, and Keldon changed his original assumptions to decide Irene Woullet was a person of exceptional taste who did not always follow the guidelines for good taste. He found her décor pleasing, a confusing contradiction.

Keldon didn't have strong feelings about her collection of art. It seemed rather ordinary. Yet he could not deny his deep delight in the beautiful, jagged colors of an impressionist piece hanging in a first-floor guest bedroom. He cooed the appropriate noises to express appreciation.

Irene summarized the piece's intention though she could not remember the artist's name without looking it up. He worked out of Arizona and was long dead. She had picked up the piece with her first husband many years ago from a local gallery there.

"I like the green shapes," Joshua said, pointing. "They remind me of fish."

She did not speak to chide him, her silence accomplished that. Keldon felt shame for Joshua and said nothing.

Joshua wheeled her from the room. Keldon still hadn't spotted the serial-killer art.

"Have we seen everything?" he politely inquired as they finished the downstairs tour.

She hesitated. "My study. I have several dozen paintings there, pieces painted by friends. It's a funny collection really, nothing impressive. I used to ask friends to create something whether they were painters or not. Most of them are awful, yet they're my favorites."

"I'd love to see them," Keldon said. Instinctively he knew this study contained the treasure he sought.

He was right.

Just a moment into the tour of the study, he spotted it, an earth with two moons in the sky, a fantastic winged creature like a griffin prancing in the foreground. He would assume it was a griffin, but the wings were terribly painted, a custard-yellow and uneven, as if banana pudding had been splattered behind the beaked creature. It was a mythological fantasy landscape, and Keldon could not deny—like it or not—he now recognized the serial killer's style. He glanced at it quickly and resumed pretending attention to the explanations regarding various paintings as Irene chuckled over her friendships and the resulting art.

"I begged my mother for years to paint me something," she said, pointing at a clumsy sailboat. "She absolutely refused. Not for my birthday, Christmas, not a single wedding anniversary. She just refused. She didn't want to embarrass herself."

"And yet, she did," Keldon said.

"Yes," Irene said and smiled. "Two days after I was diagnosed with muscular dystrophy, she appeared on my doorstep with this sailboat. That was fifteen years ago. She was a wonderful, wonderful woman."

Keldon expressed interest in the anecdotes as they made their way around the room, asking questions and chuckling when appropriate. Joshua followed, and while he brushed up against Keldon twice, Keldon couldn't tell if it was an accident or intentional. The room was not particularly large. Paintings covered almost every inch of available wall space.

Of the serial-killer art, Irene said only, "My sister painted that. Which is odd, because she was not a fantasy type. But I insisted she paint me something, and after two years of my haranguing, she reluctantly agreed. A number of friends accommodated my request, though they never painted anything else."

Keldon was careful not to express any greater interest in that piece, nothing that would give him away. Of course, he knew that Irene's sister had not painted the piece. She purchased it at a garage sale. One mystery solved—why Carolyn Woullet sent the painting to her sister.

When they finished the downstairs tour and headed toward the library once again, Joshua said, "What about upstairs? Do you want to see that art?"

Irene was quiet, and Keldon hurried to cover for the humiliation of her nurse inviting a stranger into her private space.

"I'm sure Mr. Mercer never went upstairs during his stay in your home," Keldon said. "He would not have had cause, if, in fact, he was ever here."

"The painting of the swans is up there," Joshua said. He turned to face Keldon. "It's a lot of blues and greens."

Irene struggled and said, "Yes, there's a beautiful painting upstairs. Guest bedroom. It used to hang above the fireplace years ago, so perhaps Mr. Mercer had seen it. Josh, if you would show him that one piece."

"Sure," he said and turned back toward the main staircase.

"If you wouldn't mind," she said in a sharper tone, "first guiding me to the library. And turn on the tea kettle before you go upstairs."

Joshua said, "Yeah, sure," and returned to her side to finish the task.

He pushed her to the familiar spot, and Keldon felt he perfectly understood their relationship. This was someone her daughter had hired, someone she resented but perhaps truly needed with the disease's progression. Joshua was strong and stupid, loyal to the daughter. Mrs. Woullet lived with a spy in her own household. He found himself resenting Joshua even more.

"C'mon, I'll show you." Joshua abandoned his ward, leading the way for Keldon to follow.

"Please turn on the water for the tea," she reminded him in a thin, slightly irritated voice.

"Okay, I will."

Keldon nodded apologetically to his host and waited in the hallway until Joshua returned from the kitchen.

"This way," Joshua said.

Keldon reluctantly followed Joshua in silence up the front staircase. Keldon studied Joshua's thick legs and beefy ass all the way to the top. He led Keldon to a bedroom and sauntered inside.

Keldon was surprised when Joshua turned around and said, "That's the swan painting. So what's the deal?"

"Excuse me?"

"It's just us," Joshua said, and his blank eyes registered very little interest. "Is one of these paintings worth a million dollars or something?"

"No," Keldon said.

"So what's the deal?"

Keldon stared into Joshua's face. "I don't know what the *deal* is. I just know what Mr. Mercer wants."

Keldon pretended to study the swan painting. It was nothing worthy of study, really, just some swans on a pond and their reflections. Nothing special. So he reflected on the personal attendant at his side. Keldon was unable to shake the assumption that Nurse Joshua was a few degrees slower than the rest of humanity. Irene resented his over-familiarities. He could use her distaste for Joshua to his advantage. Hint at the money troubles until she sent Joshua out of the room. Yes, he considered. That could work. He could play on this uncomfortable relationship to help her realize how much she wanted and needed that money.

He did not enjoy uncovering ways to turn this delicate situation to his advantage. But apparently it was a skill of his. Someone thought so highly of this ability to manipulate outcomes that this person recommended him to Catherine. It bothered Keldon that this was how he was known, this damning skill.

"Do you wanna kiss?" Joshua said, turning to Keldon.

"What?"

"Do you wanna make out?"

Keldon reeled in surprise. "No, I absolutely do not. Why would you think that?"

Joshua shrugged. "I think you're cute. You're pretty."

Keldon wanted to say something rude, to help the impertinent male nurse remember his role. So he did. "I think it would be disrespectful to Mrs. Woullet if we took this opportunity to make out like horny teenagers, don't you?"

Joshua said, "I dunno."

"Well, it's rude," Keldon said. "You should have a little more respect for her house."

He turned and retraced his steps down the hallway and down the staircase.

Behind him, he heard Joshua's worried voice say, "Don't tell her, okay?"

Keldon said nothing and continued at the same pace. He might be able to use Joshua's gaffe to his advantage. Keldon reminded himself that people were awful. Through and through. He showed himself back to the library where he found Mrs. Woullet reading from one of the many books surrounding her. She smiled upon seeing him.

"It's lovely," Keldon said, sitting in the chair she indicated. "I particularly love the blue highlights against the white feathers to suggest the pond's reflection. It's a lovely piece."

"Is it the one Mr. Mercer admired?"

Keldon gave his most charming shrug. "I don't know. Possibly. I'd like to request you include it in the paintings if you accept his offer."

He vaguely noted that Joshua didn't rejoin them, but heard what sounded like silverware and plates clanging together in the kitchen, indicating the nurse was preparing their afternoon refreshments.

Keldon said, "Do you have a reaction or thoughts regarding the proposal?"

"I wish I knew which piece it was," Irene said. "There are so many I would like to keep. I hate thinking of them in a basement or discarded because Mr. Mercer was only after one piece."

Keldon did not worry in the least that he may give up the identity of the painting. He shrugged off her questions and circled back to her willingness to accept the deal.

Joshua arrived with a bamboo tray laden with treats, teacups, a pot, and a small pile of lemon-colored squares covered in powdered sugar.

He set down the tray with surprising grace, no clattering, and poured the first cup.

"Well, what do you think?" Irene Woullet said, her eyes flinching and narrowing at Keldon.

Keldon paused and pretended to weigh his words. "The offer is strange, I know, but I think—"

"No," Joshua said, handing the tea to Irene. "She meant me."

Keldon almost snapped at him, an impolite retort to establish himself further in the good graces of the woman he needed to impress, but a speedy glance at his hostess showed him the big idiot nurse was correct.

Joshua continued. "'Rene, I didn't add any cream since your stomach was upset earlier. Well, it's definitely not the swan painting."

"I didn't think so," Irene said. "He was content not to see anything upstairs. Which means it's something downstairs. And good call on the cream."

Joshua turned to Keldon and said, "Cream or sugar in yours?"

Keldon was shocked to discover Joshua's whole face was wrong. It wasn't the same. It wasn't dull and stupid anymore. His eyes shone brightly, illuminating his intelligence, restoring the handsomeness to full strength.

Keldon blushed as he realized Joshua had been faking being stupid. His assumption had been wrong.

Staring Keldon down, Joshua said, "It's one of the paintings in the den."

"Are you sure?" Irene said. "I didn't see him react to anything in there."

Keldon realized both sets of eyes watched him carefully, eagerly scanning him for the smallest tell. He had been played. He blushed. He had been *played*.

"Pretty sure whatever he wants is in the den," Joshua said, turning toward the tea tray again. "After looking at all the other first-floor rooms, Keldon asked 'Is that everything?' which suggests that he still hadn't seen the painting he came here to confirm."

"Don't look so shocked, dear," Irene Woullet said, smiling and nodding at Keldon. "We're just curious as to which painting your client wants. I think I have a right to know that."

"All of them," Keldon said, adjusting to the new realization. The two of them had been working as a team, Joshua deliberately playing stupid so Keldon would focus his attention on her, allowing Joshua to better observe Keldon. It infuriated him. They'd *played* him. People were always trying to play him.

Joshua said over his shoulder, "Sugar or cream? Both?"

"Neither," Keldon said, wanting nothing from these people. But he needed the painting. He needed the money Catherine promised, which meant he could not storm out or sulk. He needed to stay.

"I don't know," Irene said, taking another long sip. "If he had already seen the painting he wanted, he could have said, 'Is that everything?' to distract us, make us think he really was curious about the whole house full of art. Do you think Keldon knows what piece he's here to acquire?"

"Definitely," Joshua said, and the firm ring irritated Keldon. That voice, that clarity so perfectly matched Joshua's obvious intellect. Keldon now blamed himself for believing in the dead-looking gaze.

Joshua handed a full teacup to Keldon and said, "Lemon square? I baked them this morning."

"No, thank you," Keldon said politely, trying to mask the coldness he felt.

"You really should try them, Keldon," Irene said earnestly. "He made them from scratch."

Joshua returned to the tray and poured a third cup for himself.

"Mr. Mercer's offer still stands," Keldon said. "Your entire household of art for the number listed in the letter."

"Yes," Irene said, "let's discuss Mr. Mercer. He's not your real backer. We checked him out."

Keldon tried his best not to react. He was aware of two sets of eyes staring at him.

She continued. "You shouldn't be surprised. A woman calls and offers you money for every piece of art in your home. You check it out. You make phone calls. There is no Mr. Mercer. He doesn't exist."

Keldon smiled while he tried to think through a response.

"He doesn't *exist*," Joshua repeated, standing with his own tea, stirring a spoon in it.

Keldon sipped to avoid answering. It was good tea, an unusual blend he did not recognize. Under other circumstances, he would have asked for its name.

"The offer stands," Keldon said. "My employer has sent me to confirm the offer in person. I know this may seem very odd to you, but I've brought legal paperwork with me confirming the offer and payment. The only requirement is that you do not discuss the sale of your artwork, any of your artwork, for one year. That's it."

"What do you think?" Irene said, staring at Keldon.

"I think my employer is odd," Keldon said, "but—"

"Nope," Joshua said, interrupting. "Still not you. She meant me. Here's what I think. He's never met Mr. Mercer."

"I never said that I had," Keldon said evenly.

"You implied you did," Joshua said. "You let us think you had spoken with him directly."

He thought of protesting, but who knew what they knew? Keldon remained silent.

Joshua spoke and watched Keldon closely for a reaction. "We lied just now. There is definitely a man named Byron Mercer. He collects art. He's a senior vice president for some mega company that's headquartered in Milwaukee, so he's a real person. But our attempts to get hold of him failed. His assistant promised she would pass along our urgent requests to return our calls. She herself didn't know anything about this art collection project."

"Mrs. Maggiarra—"

"Not her," Irene said, "Mr. Mercer's *real* assistant. I spoke with Mrs. Maggiarra at length. She passed herself off as Mr. Mercer's assistant, but she's not. You people aren't being honest with us."

"It's not polite," Joshua said, leaning back on a paisley couch with white-tasseled pillows. He took a bite from a lemon square.

"And pretending to be thick?" Keldon asked. "Telling me that there's no Mr. Mercer to see how I would react? These are lessons in politeness?"

"No, they're not," Joshua admitted. "But we're trying to figure out the game. I'm sorry I tricked you. But to be fair, you're in the middle of trying to trick Irene."

The three did not speak for a moment, letting the silence fully unfold. Keldon tried to determine where it might go next.

"You won't tell us which painting it is," Irene said, "will you?"

Keldon pretended to reflect on the answer, but he knew he would not. They would get no more clues out of him until he figured out a next step. "I have been authorized to purchase every piece of art in the house. I don't have the authority to answer your question. I'll have to confer first."

"He's good," Joshua said, tipping his cup in salute toward Keldon. "I'll give them that. They picked a good money man."

Keldon raised his eyebrows.

Joshua picked up a lemon square. "In a con, the guy who actually picks up the money is called *the money man*. It's a thing. In a con."

"Oh," Keldon said. He opened the briefcase at his feet and pulled out the legal paperwork. "I admit it's a strange offer, but completely legal. No one is trying to cheat you."

"He's handsome," Irene said, setting down her tea on a stack of books. "He dresses well, as if he represents money. That's important. Shoes are polished. He is careful about his appearance. He is handsome, right?"

"Yes," Joshua agreed. "He's got beautiful eyes. He's got those classic features. Good bones and clean planes. He's a hottie."

"Another point in Keldon's favor," Irene said, turning to face her nurse, "is that he never told on you. You gave us time alone while you finished the tea, and he never told me that you asked him to make out. He's got some dignity. Maybe some kindness in him."

"Yes," Joshua said. "He might be a good person."

Keldon blushed, resenting their talking about him like a steak. He said, "How did you know Joshua asked to make out with me? You two never communicated until he came in here with the tea set. Oh." Keldon realized the answer before either one could respond. "It was a setup. To see if I'd make out with Joshua and if I didn't, if I'd tattle on him."

"We have to know who we're dealing with," Irene said. "This much money for all my worthless paintings when all you really want is only one. It's very disconcerting. So, yes, we designed a few tests to see what we could learn about this odd situation."

"We know the painting is somewhere downstairs," Joshua said. "And I think it's in the den."

Irene cleared her throat. "I'm not convinced. "I know everyone who painted the den paintings. Why would anyone want something painted by my mother? By my husband's two children? No, Josh, we can't limit ourselves to just the den paintings, not yet. And we still don't know if Mr. Byron Mercer is really involved, because Keldon didn't give anything away. Point to *him*. But I don't think we know the whole story here either. I think this Mrs. Maggiarra knows more than she says. She did not have the phone deference for a personal assistant."

Keldon understood now that this was a game, a game in which everything he volunteered might give rise to a new suspicion or somehow inadvertently answer an existing question. He stayed quiet.

Joshua chewed a lemon bar and white powdered sugar clung to the top of his lip. Keldon noted how pretty the arch of his lip was, and instinctively, he wanted to lick the powdered sugar. Then he remembered that he hated his deceiver. Well, disliked if not hated.

Joshua caught him staring, but Keldon refused to look away. Once it was clear he wasn't embarrassed, he looked to Irene. "The offer stands."

"Would you sleep with him?" Irene asked, and Keldon blushed.

Keldon said, "I'm not ans—"

"Still not you, bud," Joshua said. "And yes, for the record, probably. I like his wiry frame, and he's sexy in a suit. But the problem with handsome guys is that they're often lazy in bed. If he's got a big dick, forget it. He'll be a terrible lay. But if he's average sized, he might be decent. Something to prove."

Keldon stood. He wanted to leave, but the idea of returning to Catherine without securing the painting meant he would never get his six figures for finishing the job. He did not know what he would do next.

"I apologize," Irene said, and now she looked embarrassed. "That was rude. Joshua and I know each other very well. We sometimes forget to show manners. You've been nothing but polite to us. Please accept my apology."

Keldon did not move.

"I apologize," Joshua said.

Keldon looked into his eyes and was surprised to find sincerity.

Joshua said, "While we're trying to trick you into revealing more about what's going on here, I forgot there's a real person in front of us. I was trying to shock you, not offend. We both went too far. Not cool."

Keldon slowly allowed himself to sit. He nodded to signify his acceptance of their apology. This could work. He could use their guilt to his advantage. "The offer?"

"Pass," Irene said. "I do not like being used or manipulated, and this feels like one of those two. You may tell Mrs. Maggiarra to discuss the situation openly or else there is no deal to be made."

"The money," Keldon said. "I was made to understand it would be advantageous to you right now, your current financial state."

"Yes," Irene said. "Dying is expensive. The house is mortgaged heavily, and I'm behind on payments. Undoubtedly foreclosure will begin within a few months. I may be dead by then. I'm progressing rapidly. It would be nice to leave Joshua a bonus—"

In a soft voice, Joshua said, "Hey."

She looked at Joshua, and Keldon could see something pass between them, a kindness, an understanding. He found himself envying their friendship.

Irene directed herself toward Keldon. "But Joshua will be fine without a financial incentive and it matters little to me whether I die in debt. So your money doesn't mean much, honestly. Your Mrs. Maggiarra has miscalculated my need."

Keldon felt the defeat. He knew it was final. He'd suffered roadblocks from the Turners and the others. He understood reluctance and recognized the games of negotiation. But this was different. This was an actual *no*.

Irene turned her attention toward Joshua. "What about the painting of the pears, the one in the kitchen?"

"The one by the back door?"

"Yes," Irene said. "That one could be famous. Maybe. We bought it on a trip. Matthew liked it."

Joshua shook his head. "I still think it's in the den."

Keldon watched them renew the debate with a sinking sense of defeat. He had to turn this to his advantage. He had to stop the finality of that *no*. Catherine had hired him to eliminate obstacles and acquire the paintings through any legal means. A few different strategies raced through his head.

"I'm sorry to be so frustrating to you," Irene said, setting down her tea. "Your trip was a waste of time."

"Not at all," Keldon said, smiling, considering the one thing he knew they did not. "I was able to confirm the desired painting is here. That was useful."

Both Joshua and Irene got quiet. Keldon was pleased to have the upper hand for a moment, even if it was slight.

"We're at an impasse," Keldon said. "My employer still wishes to buy your entire art collection."

"Which I won't sell," Irene said.

"Yes," Keldon said. His mind raced, trying to utilize a bargaining position in his negotiations, some advantage he could press, but the only thing he felt he was good at was dating. He needed to stall for more time. "But what if I…"

Dating. It was something he was good at.

"I've got an idea," Keldon said, shifting his body toward Joshua. "Go on a date with me. In Chicago. I'll pay for you to come, get you a hotel room overnight. We'll go out for dinner, and I'll spend the date trying to convince you why Mrs. Woullet should sell the paintings. You can spend the date trying to figure out which one my client wants."

Joshua barked out a laugh, and the tea wobbled over the lip of his cup, spilling into the saucer. "You're joking."

Keldon enjoyed whatever passed through Joshua to make him nervous. Didn't matter if it was attraction or just discomfort at the very idea. When you found a weakness, you exploited it.

"Are you afraid the only way you can get information out of me is to trick me?" Keldon said. "The two of you were very skilled at deceiving me. Are you afraid of an evening discussing this openly?"

"Are you sure you want to get on a high horse about deception?" Joshua asked.

Keldon shrugged. "Mrs. Maggiarra has been upfront. She wants your entire art collection. It's a legitimate offer with the one clause being you cannot discuss the sale of these paintings for a year. That's it. No tricks. The painting I came to acquire isn't worth millions. Sorry. It has value to my patron. Now, is that patron Mr. Mercer, Mrs. Maggiarra, or some other party? I don't know. I will say this. You're not my first collection. The money is real. This offer is real."

Irene frowned slightly, setting down her teacup.

"What do you say, Joshua? A night in Chicago, just you and me."

Joshua glanced at his employer. "It's rude. You should deal with Irene."

"I like it," Irene said, turning toward her friend. "If you have no strong objection, you should do this. Give yourself a night on the town. When was the last time you had an actual date?"

"It's been a while," Joshua said and glanced at Keldon. "A long while."

"Go. Have fun. See what you can learn. I do believe that our Mr. Keldon Thurman presents himself authentically, even if he represents shadowy people. You might enjoy yourself."

Joshua looked at Keldon. "He *does* have pretty eyes."

Keldon was surprised to be pleased by Joshua's remark and the idea that he would have a full date to convince Irene to sell, albeit through Joshua. Dating was his forte. Dating is what he knew. He had a better shot at gaining their cooperation over sushi and sake.

"Wait," Joshua said. "This won't be fair. Chicago is your town, your home-field advantage. I want the home-field advantage."

"You want us to go on a date here in Madison?"

"Two dates," Joshua said. "One date in Chicago and one date here in Madison."

Irene laughed. "I love this."

Keldon considered and said, "Agreed. Do you like sushi?"

* * * *

Keldon pulled over several blocks from Irene Woullet's home and called Catherine to report his findings, including their savvy attempt to trick information out of him. He avoided explaining the two-dates plan. He first wanted to hear her reaction to the overall visit.

"This is not ideal," Catherine said.

Keldon realized this was possibly the most expressive thing he had ever heard from her.

"Are you sure they don't know which painting is Merrick's?"

Keldon said, "I saw the Merrick painting. Irene Woullet collects art painted by all her friends and family. I got the impression Irene would sometimes hound them whether they wanted to paint something or not. Obviously, Carolyn Woullet bought it at the garage sale for the sole purpose of sending to Irene. It's ugly enough that you can tell an amateur painted it."

"Well, that explains something," Catherine said.

There was a silence on the phone.

"We have a few options," Keldon said. "We either tell Mrs. Woullet which painting we want, we offer more money, offer her something she can't refuse, or…"

"Yes," Catherine said sharply.

"I think the key to winning Irene Woullet is through her male nurse, her attendant. He's gay." Keldon paused. "I want to spend time alone with him. Try to soften him to the idea so he persuades Irene."

Briefly, he filled her in on the two-date plan.

"Yes, yes, whatever it takes," Catherine said. "I want that painting. Do what you have to. But nothing illegal and no threats, that sort of thing. I can't have recriminations and lawsuits later. Everything must be legal."

"Of course," Keldon said. "You've made that clear. But I want to wine and dine him. I'll need money."

Catherine said, "Money's no problem."

Only if you have it, Keldon thought, but did not speak aloud.

Chapter Four

Keldon felt nervous in a way he did not for most dates.

Most dates.

As if he dated often.

Keldon met Steven when he was twenty-one and had almost no dating experience. Steven had picked him up from a college coffee house, someplace Keldon frequented when he wanted to be seen studying. They didn't so much *date* as were instantly joined in a relationship. Keldon found himself learning how to please Steven, not just sexually, though Steven had his preferences, but also how to avoid conversations Steven disliked, how to earn his smile and affection. It was not calculated, not at first, it was pleasure.

Keldon liked Steven.

He found himself wanting to please Steven, just to make him happy. The occasional gifts were a lovely surprise, but it was the spontaneous trip to New York that made Keldon realize he could really get accustomed to dating Steven and all the accompanying perks. After a few more trips and white cloth dining at sumptuous restaurants, his burnt-toast student life seemed ridiculous and devoid of meaning. Keldon found himself accidentally growing more calculated in pleasing Steven. By the time he realized he was getting good at this manipulative skill, it was too late to turn it off.

Keldon checked his watch. Joshua would arrive in roughly an hour. The limo driver had called Keldon to confirm. Keldon had showered, shaved, dressed in black slacks, a long-sleeved silver shirt, something that would allow his eyes to sparkle in contrast. The night wasn't too chilly, warm for the last day of April, which meant wearing his custom-designed leather coat might seem too much, ostentatious even. Keldon knew he looked good in it, but as Joshua was smarter than he first appeared, Keldon didn't want to come across as trying too hard to impress.

A black stretch limo certainly fell under the category of "trying too hard to impress" but was worth the risk. Even wealthy ex-boyfriends like Steven and Aamir slipped under a powerful spell once inside a black limo, pushing every button, drinking from the lush stocked bar with childlike glee, stretching out and saying, "This is the life." Nobody was immune. Keldon wanted Joshua to feel that rush of money and power. Truth be told, he had hoped to intimidate Joshua a bit, soften him up. He didn't like being this calculated, but he didn't know how not to be.

With an hour to wait before showing up at the sushi restaurant, Keldon found himself tired of reviewing the questions he intended to ask, the self-revelations he hoped would position himself in the best light. His studio apartment required no cleaning as he did not intend to invite Joshua to his place. He had nothing to do but wait. On a lark, he sat at his computer and googled the serial killer James Wayne Merrick.

After ten years' imprisonment, Merrick was executed for his crimes in 2005. Two attempts had been made on his life by men in the general prison population, which forced the warden to assign Merrick his own private cell, his own private life. Merrick had taken up painting, mostly fantasy and science fiction scenes, to soothe his savage soul. And it *was* a savage soul. Mr. James Wayne Merrick had developed a fondness for picking up female hitchhikers in the rain. Mostly teens. Some older, their twenties or early thirties. He wasn't too particular about gender or age, though, and indulged in killing men and children when he could not find young women. One or two kids' bikes were found abandoned alongside a semi-deserted road during the rain, but the kids themselves were never found until the story broke in early 1990.

While studying the Wikipedia page devoted to Merrick, he scrolled past the paragraphs summarizing tortures and probable fates of his victims. Keldon didn't want to know. He didn't understand why someone—anyone—would be fascinated to know those details, how that could enrich one's life. The bodies were found buried near a crude hunting shanty owned by Merrick. The first body was discovered by accident. A vacationing family's dog returned to their camp fire from the forest with an odd-shaped bone.

Keldon felt he'd read enough. He closed the page and tried not to dwell on his own connection to this killer through Mrs. Maggiarra.

He didn't like collecting Merrick's art for Catherine Maggiarra, but what could he do? He didn't need to recalculate his finances or reflect more on Chicago's expensive cost of living. He had spent too many hours incessantly worrying about money. He knew those well-worn treads in his brain.

He considered googling Joshua again but didn't see how it would reveal more details than it had the first time. It had, in fact, yielded very little. No Facebook page. No LinkedIn associations. Keldon had paid to track Joshua's high school graduation records, which revealed nothing more than his dates of graduation. He was so intrigued by the lack of information he requested Catherine put her anonymous investigators on Joshua Tyson Greene. Her mysterious sources found biological information, parents and a sister in Denver, but very little else. He owned a single credit card that he used infrequently. He rented a home in Madison.

Keldon decided to leave for the restaurant, unwilling to start another web search or begin a task that might distract him from the evening's intentions. He left his Logan Square brownstone, divided into the maximum number of apartments possible. Keldon sometimes wondered if they had converted broom closets into apartments as it seemed there were way too many units squeezed out of this building. It always came down to money— how much developers could make off apartment dwellers. His garden apartment was small and leaked rain through faulty window caulking. But he dared not complain or exhaust the last of the landlord's patience. Eviction always seemed imminent.

* * * *

Tiger Sushi, one of the north side's exquisite pleasures, was not terribly far, just three stops north on the El's brown line. Aamir loved sushi and back when he still loved Keldon, Aamir had introduced the two. For a split second, Keldon had hesitated in making the reservation, wondering if he could possibly run into Aamir, but decided he simply didn't care. He did not hate Aamir for dumping him at the O'Hare airport, communicating him via text the trip was cancelled as was their relationship. Well, maybe he hated Aamir a little. But he wanted nothing to do with the man, not to see him, not to experience him. Keldon would not create a scene in a restaurant if Aamir happened to prefer sushi tonight. He would do his best to remain unnoticed.

Keldon arrived with a half-hour to spare, and after confirming the reservation with the Tiger Sushi maître d', he called the limo driver to confirm Joshua's arrival time. Keldon waited outside, wishing he hadn't given up smoking, another expensive habit he found himself unable to maintain after rich boyfriends left him. He passed the time wandering down Clark Street to nearby restaurants, studying their menus posted on the front windows.

A black stretch limo pulled in front of the restaurant within fifteen minutes of the appointed hour, and Keldon self-consciously brushed himself off, not sure if it accomplished anything but desperate to be doing something other than staring, waiting for his guest to emerge. When the driver opened the door, Keldon fixed a pleasant smile on his face, somewhat plastic but also somewhat sincere, a smile he hoped hid his anxiousness.

Joshua stepped out, and the smile faded.

Joshua had gotten a haircut, styling the shaggy mop of brown locks into something short and bristly, something you might want to run your fingers through. The sides of his head almost looked shaved. The four-day stubble that had made him appear dopey and unkempt had also disappeared, replaced with a masculine dark shadow around his jawline. He smiled at Keldon, and although Keldon knew it was his job to smile back, he could only stare. Joshua wore a green silk shirt hanging over black jeans, a dark seaman's coat unbuttoned, and black gym shoes. The shimmering green drew Keldon's attention. He couldn't stop staring at the expansive chest, the ripples made by Joshua's strolling closer.

"A bit much," Joshua said, indicating the limo with an incline of his head.

Keldon didn't remember Joshua looking this way: impressive, hot. Keldon remembered he liked the shape of the man, and he remembered the intelligence in his eyes that had fooled him, but Joshua was an obstacle to his success, not a real person until this moment. He realized if he had met Joshua dressed like this, he would have never invited him on a date. Not someone this handsome.

Keldon stammered out the words "Thank you," though he wasn't sure they applied or he couldn't remember what he wanted to say. He blushed hard, and suddenly the situation felt like more of a date than he wanted it to be. *Business*, he reminded himself. *This is business.*

"You know how wasteful a limo is, right? The carbon emissions?" Despite Joshua's pointed question, Keldon could see a glint of friendliness. It was a rebuke but not a sharp one.

"I wanted to impress you," Keldon said, blushing.

"Mmmm," Joshua said, stepping closer. "Next time, buy me a bouquet of kale."

Joshua excused himself to use the washroom, entering the restaurant, and Keldon discussed post-dinner plans with the limo driver. Keldon also went inside and stood by the front podium, trying to remember the salient points he wanted to cover tonight. He had a plan. He had to remember the plan. When Joshua joined him at his side, Keldon had the fleeting impression of a minister's pulpit and Joshua having just walked down the wedding aisle to meet him.

Keldon's eyes widened when the maître d' said, "Are you ready?"

They followed the host through the dimly lit environment with its Japanese-influenced décor, polished onyx tables and interior walls crisscrossed with katana blades. Throughout the large dining area, crinkled paper screens wafted from the ceiling adorned with Japanese characters, bottom-lit with orange floor lights, finishing the impression of sophisticated, muscular power. Keldon snuck a glance, and Joshua grinned in his direction. Keldon forgot what reaction he had hoped for.

They were formally introduced to their table, a gleaming black reflection interrupted only by bamboo place settings and a simple paper candle holder promising flickering fire inside. The constant hum of steady dinner conversation flowed everywhere around them, occasionally punctuated with a silvery laugh or boisterous remark that de-escalated to normal volume after cresting like a wave.

"It's beautiful," Joshua said. "I can see why you chose this place. I like the scrolls on the wall. Glad I dressed up."

"Yes, I love this place," Keldon said. "Do you eat sushi much?"

"Rarely. They sell it in the deli area at Co-op, but I never trust it. I'd only eat it from a high-end place like this. And I don't eat high-end on a nurse's salary, so you should order for both of us. I'll eat anything but squid and calamari. Calamari seems like it's just basically squid in drag."

Keldon chuckled and felt glad. He wanted to impress Joshua with his ordering prowess and perhaps gain his trust. He hoped that if he could gain Joshua's trust in small matters, food recommendations, dinner conversation, and impress him with a limo and night spent in a gorgeous hotel, Joshua might trust him in bigger matters. Or at least transfer some goodwill to Keldon and help persuade Irene to sell the paintings.

Keldon led the conversation on various sushi possibilities, discussing textures and flavors, learning the degree of spiciness Joshua preferred and discussing types of fish used to create exotic presentations.

"I never really got into sushi," Joshua said. "Maybe hold back on the octopus stuffed inside a squid wrapped in a shark. But other than that, I'll defer to your expertise."

"California rolls are always a safe bet," Keldon said. "They're simple. Delicious. Well, if you like avocado."

"I do. Order them. What else is tasty?"

Keldon spoke effortlessly about sushi preparation, the way flavors were introduced without cooking, which fish more easily combined with unique flavors such as ginger and wasabi. Joshua asked questions, seeming intrigued by Keldon's pairings. Discussion of food, food textures, and Chicago restaurants dominated the conversation until the waiter brought edamame and their seaweed salads.

"Shall we play a game?" Joshua said, popping the first bean from its pod. "Ow. The edamame is hot."

"What game?"

"Hang on," Joshua said, shifting the bean from one side of his mouth to the other. "Seriously hot." After taking a sip of water, Joshua spoke again. "A game to see who reveals the most or least about tonight's awkward conversations. It's called Truth or Date."

Keldon paused and considered this. "I assume it's like truth or dare."

"Yes, very similar. But instead of a *dare*, you answer a question about your dating history, who you would date, sex, anything related to your personal life. Either way, you're always answering a question with the truth, either about this weird painting situation or about yourself."

Keldon popped his own edamame and tried not to show how right Joshua was—the beans were sizzling his mouth. "I'll pass on the game. It's not my place to reveal much about my client's motives, and I have a feeling your first truth question will be 'which painting?'"

Joshua flashed a warm smile. "I promise I won't ask that. I may ask for hints—no, I can see by your face you don't like that either. Okay, no clue-asking. Plus, you can always pass on a truth question and take a date question. It'll be fun."

Keldon reconsidered. He had plotted a careful approach to the awkward topic before them, but he honestly could not imagine how well the conversation would go. Much was at stake, and he didn't know how to uncover answers he wanted. This game might work. Plus, it was Joshua's idea, and Keldon knew that if Joshua felt in control, he might unwittingly find himself more involved, more ready to collaborate. It might be worth the risk.

"I'll take truth," Keldon said.

"Which painting is it you guys want?" Joshua said. Upon seeing the surprised irritation on Keldon's face, he quickly amended his words. "Aw, c'mon. That was funny. I was being Mr. Funny Guy. Relax. That's not my real question. My real question is why you're doing this. Why you're this art collector guy."

"It's my job."

"Yeah, but you could work other jobs. Why are you doing *this* job. What's in it for you?"

"Money," Keldon said without giving the matter much thought. "Artistic acquisitions pays well."

Joshua considered this and broke another bean in half. "You have to reveal something when you play Truth or Date. You have to make the question worthwhile. You can't just say that you work for money because everyone in the world does that. I want to know why this particular job as opposed to working as an engineer or stealing diamonds as an international jewel thief."

Keldon chuckled. "Stealing diamonds?"

Joshua shrugged. "It's a living."

Keldon considered his reasons for working this particular job and how much he might share with his dinner guest. The truth was humbling, humiliating, but it might also help Joshua let down his guard as well. Strategic vulnerability. The gin martini he sipped, and Joshua's eyes, might also have influenced his decision.

"I'm not good at anything," Keldon said. "I didn't finish college. I don't have any real-world skills. I have worked temp jobs and retail and hated both. This job offer came along, and it pays really well. So it truly is about the money for me. But it also happens that I am not skilled at anything else and floundering with what to do with my life."

"Oh," Joshua said and stopped. Keldon could see by his face he was startled by what he had heard and the playful, teasing edge to the game vanished.

"Thank you," Joshua said and got quiet. "I'm sorry. I didn't mean for this to get so…deep. We don't have to play."

"Hey, you can't quit now," Keldon said, feeling good about how the tables had turned in his favor. He flashed Joshua a smile. "Not when it's my turn. Truth or date?"

"Date," Joshua said, relieved. "Ask me anything about dating."

"Why did you agree to come on this date?"

Joshua chuckled. "Free limo ride?"

Keldon arched his eyebrows, and the meaning was clear. *I showed you my truth, you show me yours.*

Joshua blushed. "I don't get asked out very much. I don't date. I mean, I *do* get asked out sometimes. I'm—I'm different in a way that turns guys off. I don't eat out at restaurants. I try not to use much electricity. I don't go to movies or play mini-golf or things that people do on dates. I try to live off the grid. I have a regular job, but I don't own a car, and if I can't take public transportation to get there, I don't go. It's weird, I know. I think I'm attractive enough, physically, but after one or two dates, guys decide I'm not worth the effort. I'm too quirky. And not the good quirky. Nobody wants to date the gay Amish guy."

Keldon hadn't expected that answer. "Amish?"

"No. I'm not even religious. But my lifestyle is similar in some ways. The last guy I had a few dates with called me 'gay Amish.' It wasn't a compliment."

"Okay, but that doesn't answer my question. Why did you agree to *this* date?"

Joshua sipped his own drink, taking his time. "I like who I am. I'm committed to the way I live. It's not like I'm morally opposed to people going to movies and stuff. But it gets lonely, being this weirdo who tries to live by candlelight. A limo, fancy sushi restaurant…none of this is who I am now. I'm mostly okay with that because I chose this life. But I thought it would be fun to pretend—for one night—this could be me, this could be my life. Fancy date. Handsome guy waiting for me in Chicago."

Keldon couldn't resist teasing. "You think I'm handsome?"

Joshua laughed his nervousness away. "That wasn't your question. I answered the one you asked."

Both men laughed a little, a friendly laugh. They had established they both could express vulnerability in the other's presence, a first-date milestone achieved.

The California rolls arrived, removing pressure for the game's second round. Joshua experimented with chopsticks but eventually said, "Fuck it," and picked up the rolls with his fingers. Keldon followed suit. He had no problem with chopsticks but didn't want Joshua to feel ill at ease. It was amazing how Joshua's dating confession changed his perspective. Keldon tried to focus on the evening's agenda—convincing Joshua to convince Irene to sell the paintings—but now he found himself wanting to entertain his guest, to make sure one of his infrequent dating adventures was a delight, an evening he could remember. He scolded himself to remember the money. Keep the money in focus.

But Joshua was goofy, grinning while chewing. And when his eyes went wide with terror, Keldon laughed, realizing Joshua had overused the wasabi.

"I warned you," Keldon said, "I told you not to use much."

Joshua flailed about in helpless surprise, his eyes watering, and flapped the napkin at his side, the white flag of surrender.

Keldon laughed again.

After the wasabi drama had calmed down and Joshua dried his eyes, they resumed their consumption, occasionally commenting on the freshness of the avocado and Keldon explaining the spices that made each bite taste special.

Joshua said, "You know a lot about sushi."

Keldon shrugged. "I dated a sushi enthusiast once. He taught me."

"Okay," Joshua said, "Truth or date?"

Keldon did not hesitate. "Truth."

"Okay," Joshua said, picking at the remains of his seaweed salad. "Cards on the table. What's the deal with this crazy painting offer?"

Keldon had wondered if the conversation might head in this direction and took a deep breath, unsure how to answer.

"Tell me whatever you can," Joshua said. "I'm not asking you to betray some big secret you can't reveal or whatever, but what the fuck is this? This isn't normal. You don't show up at someone's house and offer to buy every painting they own. It's weird, right? You know it's weird."

"It's weird," Keldon admitted. "I know that."

"So what can you tell me?"

"The offer is legitimate. It's not a trick." Keldon had considered he might have to reveal additional details to secure Joshua's help, so he was ready to share. But he didn't want it to come out too easily. He wanted Joshua to feel as though he was getting the inside scoop. "I've been acquiring art for two months. Yours is the fifth acquisition. Other people have received offers like the one extended to Mrs. Woullet, but no one was offered as much money as she was."

"Why not?"

"Because she's dying," Keldon said and watched Joshua flinch. "Whoever is paying my salary is rich and they felt bad for her situation."

Joshua seemed to digest this. Keldon's saltwater eel with yuzu zest and Joshua's caterpillar rolls arrived while Keldon finished his answer. Both men used the waiter's interruption to take a moment to reflect on the exchange.

Joshua asked, "Is this art really for Mr. Mercer? What's his deal?"

Keldon now knew the story, the relationship with Mr. Mercer. He had secured Catherine's permission to reveal more truth. She had grown concerned about too much misrepresentation during the acquisition and had emphasized once again everything Keldon did must be legal.

"Mrs. Maggiarra used to work for the same company where Mr. Mercer works. In fact, he was one of her bosses. The vice president she reported to. He does collect art. She's long since retired, and when she wanted to start a collection of her own, she approached him and asked permission to use his name. She doesn't want anyone to know the art is for her personal collection."

"Why?"

Keldon stopped and waited until Joshua looked him in the eye. "This sure is a long Truth or Date question."

"It is," Joshua said. "And I appreciate that you answered everything to the best of your ability. You're a lot more…I dunno, honest about all this than I expected. I appreciate that. I like you more than I thought I would."

Keldon thought about snarking out a "Gee, thanks," but the expression of sincerity on Joshua's face made him stop. He stared into Joshua's green eyes, and the shimmery reflection of his green silk shirt caught his attention again. This was a big deal for Joshua. A big date. He was being kind and sincere. Keldon felt his snarkiness melt and something warmer take its place.

"Plus you warned me about the wasabi," Joshua said, a sly grin replacing his expression. "Even though I didn't listen."

The two men laughed and clinked their glasses together, another silent toast between them. They traded sushi, sampling each other's, and did their best to describe the texture and taste while stealing subtle glances.

"Truth or date," Joshua said, "your turn to ask me something."

Keldon smiled and said, "Truth or date?"

"Truth."

"Tell me about this lifestyle thing of yours, the lack of electricity and why you do it. Also, without going into too much detail, I want to know if you use indoor plumbing."

Joshua laughed heartily, and Keldon thrilled to elicit a reaction like this. But then he started worrying. Was he trying to make Joshua laugh to delight him or to manipulate him? He wasn't sure, but even *considering* the question made him feel dirty.

"I've always been fascinated by pioneers," Joshua said. "How they lived, how they survived in the wilderness. I used to read every single book I could find on the subject. I'm not sure I want to live that way, skinning rabbits and—"

Joshua interrupted himself. "Wait. You didn't ask anything about Irene or the paintings."

Keldon shook his head. "No. Do you mind if I use up the rest of this wasabi? We can ask our waiter for more."

Joshua cocked his head. "Are you sure you want to waste your truth question asking me about how I live?"

Keldon smiled. "I'm sure."

This time, Keldon knew he felt dirty. He knew the game he played. It was a long-term strategy, one that almost always paid off with both Aamir and Steven. Express fascination with the man's interests, using deep questions and integrating information already learned, and build the trust. Keldon felt worse than before, dirtier, more slimy. He had been enjoying his time with Joshua, but he didn't know how to switch off the ability to get what he wanted. The ability to work a date. He hated himself a little bit and wondered if it would ever be possible to ignore these mercenary dating skills.

Joshua said, "You're really interested?"

Keldon lowered his eyes, suddenly immersed in the application of wasabi to the mango roll Joshua had shared. "I am."

Joshua explained his simple lifestyle, the carbon footprint he hoped to reduce. He mowed his lawn and planted flowers every summer, just like his neighbors. But he collected rainwater in his backyard and made jams and jellies all summer to barter for services. He biked everywhere he could around Madison and even moderated an online forum for those new to the going-green lifestyle. Yes, he knew it was funny that he moderated an online forum while living this lifestyle. He got the irony. And he made his own candles.

"But you use an indoor toilet."

Joshua smiled. "I do."

"And shower."

"Yes. I'm not exactly a purist."

"The pioneers will be disappointed in you."

"They are," Joshua conceded. "Two months ago, I ate Kentucky Fried Chicken. I really craved their mashed potatoes and gravy. I'm pretty sure the pioneers would be pissed off about that."

Keldon tsked him. "KFC? *Really?*"

"Hey, if the Donner party had a KFC nearby, they wouldn't have resorted to cannibalism."

Keldon tipped his water glass toward Joshua. "Ever thought about changing your name to Jebediah? It sounds more like a pioneer name."

Joshua laughed. "All the time."

Keldon said, "Does Jebediah prefer original recipe or extra-crispy?"

They finished dinner without any further Truth or Date, just conversation. Keldon found himself surprised to be growing interested in Joshua's strange lifestyle, fascinated by the self-created difficulties and Joshua's commitment. To live with minimal electricity? Constrained within the range of public transportation and bicycle? In random moments when he remembered the date's true agenda, his attempt to get Joshua to influence Irene, the words *filthy whore* snapped into his consciousness, surprising him, said in the voice of the man who he once permitted to rent his body.

Keldon felt sad, though he tried not to show it. He didn't want to feel like a filthy whore. Not while dating, not while collecting serial-killer art. He was tired of feeling ashamed.

After the obligatory complaints about overeating, Keldon called the limo driver and asked him to pick them up. Keldon settled the bill, tipping generously, and the two men strolled past the flickering paper lanterns as they navigated tables to the restaurant front.

"Where next, boss?" Joshua asked.

"Hold your horses, Jebediah," Keldon said.

Once comfortably ensconced in the limo's backseat, nestled in warm leather and listening to the soft croonings of instrumental jazz, Keldon couldn't help but ask, "Doesn't riding in a limo go against everything you believe in, everything you're trying to do with your life?"

"Yes, absolutely."

Joshua hesitated, and in the dark, Keldon imagined him blushing. Finally, Joshua continued. "I would never rent a limo on my own. The carbon footprint is inexcusable. In fact, I plan on taking a bus back to Madison tomorrow. I can't justify a second trip in this. But at the same time—and I don't want to sound like the country bumpkin—I never rode in a limo, not ever. Well, my grandmother's funeral. I was a pallbearer. This might be my only chance to enjoy an insane luxury like this."

The two men said nothing, just watched Chicago pedestrians peer into the tinted glass hoping to see some local celebrity.

"Sometimes it's good to take a vacation from yourself," Joshua said, and the discussion was closed.

For many blocks the limo drove very slow, stuck in Chicago traffic, and the two men stared out the window. Keldon attempted to point out local highlights as they approached Boystown. Joshua grunted but did not express any additional interest in leaving the limo, which was fine with Keldon. He dreaded the idea of taking Joshua to a gay bar, potentially losing his date's attention amongst all the eye candy. A few blocks later, the limo shrugged off the tedium of local traffic and slid effortlessly onto the graceful Lake Shore Drive, merging with the hundreds of other cars speeding across the wide highway, Chicago's eastern perimeter.

The city was at its most impressive from this perspective, the powerful, stocky skyscrapers with strong shoulders, electricity bursting proudly from almost every window. The recognizable shapes of the Sears Tower and John Hancock building appeared as they raced down the curvy highway, and Keldon repeatedly glanced at Joshua for any trace of being impressed. He found nothing he might recognize as awe.

"It's pretty," Keldon murmured.

"Definitely," Joshua said. "Stunning. It reminds me of New York."

"You've been?"

"Worked there for a few years."

Keldon found himself more than surprised. "You're kidding? You don't talk like you're from New York."

"Thank you," Joshua said, but added nothing more.

The rosy glow of Chicago's downtown buildings comforted Keldon. He felt safe and protected knowing they were here. He didn't understand people who were intimidated by big cities. All the people nearby, all the infrastructure of buildings and roads and lights… you could never be alone in a city this large. It wasn't possible.

"Your call as to our next activity," Keldon said. "We could go walk around Millennium Park and visit The Bean, we could go clubbing, or we could go to a piano bar downtown if you like. If you're in the mood for late-night theater, we just head back north—"

"Let's dance," Joshua said. "I haven't ever been dancing in Chicago."

Keldon liked that option, as long as it was a straight club downtown where he would not suffer too much competition. Keldon wanted Joshua to see him spin and move, let Joshua see him sweat and work the floor. He didn't get to dance much with older boyfriends. They were too self-conscious about dancing with an early-twentysomething man.

"Is it too early?" Joshua asked, looking at the time on his cell phone.

Keldon felt shock. "Wait, you have a *smartphone*?"

"For work. And emergencies," Joshua said. "Work pays for it. I don't spend much time downloading apps or texting."

"KFC and now this? Jebediah—" Keldon shook his head. "—if you can't commit, we're gonna take your cattle away and replace them with Netflix."

Joshua laughed. "I actually had a Netflix account three years ago."

Keldon felt good about himself. "Let's go to the hotel and check you into your room. Then we'll go out."

"Sure," Joshua said with a snarky grin. "Let's see the roach motel and its cum-stained sheets."

Keldon snickered and inwardly smiled with satisfaction.

When the limo stopped in front of Chicago's famous Drake Hotel, Joshua got very apologetic. "You didn't have to put me up *here*," he said, almost stammering. "I could have stayed anywhere."

The two men emerged from the back seat onto the sidewalk.

Keldon said, "Do you have an overnight bag in the trunk?"

Joshua barely answered, staring at the imposing stone façade and at the very top, the enormous scripted hotel name, pink glowing letters visible for miles away. Down the street, tall gray buildings conferred regarding city business at heights far above them, and yet the scent in the air was predominantly spring, the clean raw lake smell, the unfurling green trees spaced along the city block scenting the air with the promise of warm weather.

Keldon carried Joshua's small duffel bag while Joshua stared at the uniformed bellmen, the white horse-drawn carriage awaiting a romantic couple, the imposing stone hotel with its thick concrete arms.

Joshua turned to Keldon. "You did not have to do this. Seriously."

Keldon smiled. "C'mon. Let's get you checked in."

Keldon felt a certain pride as if he himself had orchestrated the hotel's construction. He was banking on Joshua's awe. Keldon pushed through the gold revolving doors, eager to observe Joshua's reaction to the glamorous interior. Aamir had booked a night for the two of them there once, three months before the airport dump.

It bothered Keldon how much he thought of both Aamir and Steven, especially while on a date with a hot nurse, but almost all of his adult life had been shaped dating those two men.

Joshua contained his enthusiasm but could not fully mask it, quietly gasping at the vastness of its ballroom-sized lobby, the crystal chandeliers that looked like an exploded iceberg. He stopped to touch velvety pink orchids bunched in a tall crystal flute atop one of the many polished mahogany tables.

"Those orchids are real," he said in a quiet voice to Keldon as they approached the front desk.

Keldon nodded. "I'm not surprised."

"And that enormous table should be at King Arthur's court," Joshua said.

"Oh, please," Keldon said. "Why waste it on a bunch of straight guys drinking beer and questing?"

Joshua whispered in his ear, "How do you know they were straight?"

Keldon grinned and felt himself redden.

Check-in proceeded like every other hotel, although perhaps with more niceties and special courtesy on behalf of the hotel staff.

When asked if he had ever stayed in the Drake Hotel, Keldon said, "No," because he wanted the gracious employee to explain its many amenities but thought it would be rude to point directly at Joshua and say, "He's never been here."

During the entire explanation—the first-floor designer shops, the exquisite workout facilities, the many attractions literally steps away—Joshua's gaze never stopped zinging around the lobby. While Keldon and the employee discussed room-service hours, Joshua stared at the enormous white pillars at the carved sculpture decorating the ceiling's edge.

On their way to the elevator, Joshua said, "Have you really never been here before?"

"I stayed here once."

"Oh." Joshua paused. "Truth or date?"

Keldon chuckled. "Truth."

"Why do you always choose *truth* instead of *date*?"

The two men had the oak-lined elevator to themselves. Joshua traced his fingers over the intricately carved braid pattern at each panel's edge.

"Just my preference, I guess," Keldon said. "So what's the question?"

"That was the question," Joshua said. "Why do you always choose truth? Why is it you don't want to talk about dating? It's the easiest way to avoid telling me things you don't want me to know about the painting."

The elevator pinged quietly when they reached the twenty-ninth floor, and silently the doors slid open, revealing new luxuries to be absorbed. Joshua seemed to take it in eagerly, leaping out to touch the wallpaper and the orchids on this floor.

Just when Keldon had hoped he had forgotten the question, Joshua turned and asked again. "Why do you always choose truth?"

Keldon led the walk toward the room. "I don't like to talk about my dating past. I'm not…I'm not proud."

Joshua joined him at his side. The hallways were wide enough for the two men to walk side by side with space between them. "Did you date a lot?"

"No, not really. Two ex-boyfriends."

"Were they horrible?"

"No, not at all. They were very often kind. But they liked me because I was young and stupid. And when I wasn't either of those anymore, they ended it."

Joshua reflected on this. "So basically, I'm not old enough to be your type."

"I didn't mean that." Keldon found himself blushing. He wished they could keep walking side by side, but they had arrived at the room. "I don't know if I have a type. I don't think so. But you're…you're…"

He thought he would die of embarrassment if he couldn't find a way to save this conversation. He stuck the key card into the slot, and turned the handle when the light flickered green. But he didn't want to go into the room with this conversation unfinished. He wanted to watch Joshua's delight upon seeing the room, which meant he couldn't be focused on his own ex-boyfriends.

Keldon said, "I didn't know who I was and what I wanted. I enjoyed them, and I let them take care of me to the point of ignoring school and not figuring out what I wanted in life. Now I'm twenty-nine and have no skills, no college, no plans. I don't hate them, but I don't like talking about my former dating life because it just reminds me how I fucked things up. It's easier to blame them than to accept the responsibility I let it unfold that way."

He looked up to see if there was scorn or contempt in Joshua's eyes. Joshua tried to live off the grid. He didn't need anyone. Keldon had just admitted to being a parasite, and the shame he felt boiled under his collar.

Joshua's face showed nothing, no discernible reaction, but it got closer, then closer, until Keldon found himself being kissed, tenderly kissed, an elongated kiss, not terribly wet or sticky, just the right amount of pressure to silently communicate, *I heard you*.

"There," Joshua said, pulling away. "Did that make you forget your ex-boyfriends for a moment?"

Keldon blinked in surprise.

Joshua pushed the door open and strolled inside. Keldon followed.

The suite was every bit as sumptuous as the manager had promised over the phone. Two plush gray couches faced each other, framing a glass and gold coffee table between them. A gold replica of the Sears Tower, now named something else Keldon refused to acknowledge, rose majestically from the glass top. A luxury wooden desk with an executive leather chair framed the wall with the most windows, windows overlooking the red-taillight glow from the maze of city streets below. Not a single street noise could be heard; the room was perfectly soundproofed. Joshua touched the couches, walked to the marble counter above the anterior room's bar, and gazed up at the gold sashes swinging from window to window.

"This is too much." Joshua's voice contained something humble, something sad.

"Can I make us a drink?" Keldon said.

He felt that the room was having the desired effect, wearing down Joshua's resistance, and once again he chided himself for feeling a slight thrill his agenda was getting accomplished. *You're a dirty whore*, he told himself and then immediately ignored the silent damning.

Trying to lighten the shame he felt in his heart, Keldon said, "Nice kiss, by the way. Your lips are really soft."

"Don't," Joshua said as Keldon reached for the cut crystal glasses on the built-in shelving. "Don't make us drinks. I can't do this."

Keldon said, "Well, they must have something here you like. Some cocktail."

"No," Joshua said. "I can't. I thought it would be fun to come to Chicago on your dime, or Mrs. Maggiarra's, and get a fancy dinner, stay in a nice hotel. I thought it would be fun."

"It's not?"

Joshua walked to one of the gray couches and sat. He pulled a gray pillow with gold tassels to hold in front of his stomach. "I'm not going to try to convince Irene to sell her paintings. It doesn't matter what you say tonight. I won't do it."

Keldon let that settle. It wasn't what he wanted to hear, of course, but was he truly surprised? Did he honestly think a limo ride and sushi would change Joshua's mind to convince his friend Irene? In addition, Joshua's expression of honesty was perfect. Refreshing. It made Keldon like Joshua even more. Besides, this wasn't the end. It was just the middle.

"How about if I make us something like a Cosmo?" Keldon said. "There's vodka and cranberry juice in the fridge. There's no triple sec, but we could add some orange juice as a substitute."

"I'm not kidding." Joshua looked at Keldon mournfully. "I'm not going to convince her to sell you her paintings."

"I heard you." Keldon waited until Joshua looked up. "I know. You're not going to convince Irene. But you could tell her I'm not an asshole and that I warned you about the wasabi."

Joshua huffed a small chuckle.

"Joshua," Keldon said, "I didn't honestly think you'd go out on one date with me and convince her to sell. That's not realistic. But the offer is legitimate. I honestly don't know what Mrs. Maggiarra is doing or why she wants what she wants, whether for her or someone else, but Irene isn't getting screwed. The painting Mrs. Maggiarra wants isn't worth much money. She paid $4,000 for the last one, so Irene really is getting a generous offer. But if you tell Irene Mrs. Maggiarra's offer is real and there isn't a catch, that would be enough. Let her decide on her own what to do."

Joshua considered this from the couch and released the pillow from its captivity. When he looked at Keldon again, Keldon could see the burden had been lifted.

He smiled. "Two dates. We're going on two dates, not one."

"Sorry?"

"You said we were going on one date. I'm reminding you it's two."

Keldon nodded and felt himself secretly pleased. "Two dates. Sushi in Madison."

"Pot roast," Joshua said. "I'm going to make you a pot roast. But first, you're making me an imitation Cosmo. I want to hold a fancy drink and stroll around this room. God, I haven't even seen the bedroom yet."

Joshua bounced off the couch and jogged to the glass french doors leading to the second room.

As Keldon reached for the vodka, he heard, "*Holy shit.*"

Keldon chuckled. It was hard to reconcile the idea of Joshua living in New York City yet being this impressed with the Drake Hotel. Who was the real Joshua? A jaded, former New Yorker? A simple pioneer from Wisconsin? Keldon didn't care. He told himself it didn't matter, that Joshua was his date for tonight, and now that he was no longer under the self-imposed obligation to try to manipulate Joshua, he could relax and enjoy himself.

Joshua poked his head from the bedroom door to say, "By the way, everyone calls me Josh."

* * * *

The club Keldon selected wasn't exclusive. It wasn't the best of the best, the hottest nightclub that only the experienced clubbers knew about. He took Josh to the Castle, a Chicago tradition back when it was named Excalibur. A face-lift in 2012 gentrified the raucous club into a more lucrative avenue, splitting the nightclub into a pub, cabaret catering to bachelorette parties, a dance club, and another overflow dance club called the Dome Room. Keldon was sure he would not be impressed, but he banked on the hope Joshua would be.

While the club boasted the hottest DJs and laser light show, Keldon couldn't help but view Excalibur's recent remodeling through the lens he viewed all of life: money. Excalibur wasn't satisfying its investors, so they took a Chicago landmark and divided it, gave it big fake tits, a jiggly ass, and said, "Go make

Daddy more money." It was the same with the Sears Tower, a Chicago landmark renamed because someone with more money wanted their name pissed in the snow. Keldon hated money's grasping influence, and he hated how much he wanted more of it.

Keldon wondered if all twenty-nine-year-olds felt this jaded. Probably. Maybe. Maybe not those with careers and life plans. Worst of all, Keldon knew he was part of it, stuck in the money-grubbing machine. If someone tossed $100 bills from the club balcony tonight, would he dive for them? Yup. He would. Just a few minutes ago, Joshua—or rather, Josh—suggested they walk to the club as it was only fifteen minutes away on North Dearborn. Keldon argued they should take the limo. How often do you pull up in front of a Chicago nightclub in a black stretch limo?

Josh laughed and caved immediately. "I won't live long enough to erase tonight's carbon footprint."

As the limo approached their destination, Keldon found himself looking forward to expensive club drinks and dancing. Since Mrs. Maggiarra would pay for the evening's expenses, he intended to enjoy himself. Keldon didn't like admitting that part of him enjoyed being kept. He even welcomed it. He now understood the risks of being a kept man, but a night off from worrying about money was a welcome relief. Tonight, Catherine Maggiarra would be his sugar momma, and he did not mind.

He rose from the back seat of the limousine with grace, mindful not to look around or make eye contact with anyone who might express curiosity as to who just arrived. He stood by the car door and offered his hand to Josh, who took it, and Keldon could tell from the sparkle in his grin that it pleased him, this entrance, this splash. Josh didn't act like a city mouse, but he wasn't a country mouse either, which Keldon found fascinating. He was all country at this moment, bashfully grinning at the purple-tinged light and thump-pounding beats exploding over the Chicago sidewalk. From inside, a group howl interrupted the thumping musical narrative. The two men found themselves sprayed with neon colors, like two wealthy hippies who showed up in tie-dye.

Keldon approached the gatekeeper, not the bouncer, but the true gatekeeper who stood in the shadows, barely out of sight but always with a commanding view of the line to get in. He hoped he could pull off a bribe as well as his ex-boyfriends, and had bills at the ready. An old-fashioned bribe seemed to be the best chance of success, so he strolled to the gentleman with confidence and asked if he might impress a first date with a quick entrance to the interior club, Palladium. The gentleman felt the press of soft, folded money in his hand before he could reply and when he looked down, he said, "Nice. Old school. Kinda a shitty tip for Saturday night in Chicago, but I like your confidence. And you're cute, which is good for business."

When asked whom to let in, Keldon indicated Josh with an inclination of his head and tried to mask the humiliation he felt at undertipping. Yet another indicator he did not belong in an expensive, moneyed world. He was a pretender, someone who did not understand money's true nature.

The gatekeeper, an expensive suit-wearing man in his thirties, made a show of jogging down the front steps and bowing slightly before Josh, who grinned with unanticipated pleasure, and followed the suit to the red velvet rope.

"How cool," Josh said in a murmur as the rope parted to gain them access amid the groans of long-suffering patrons still waiting.

It took some time to navigate the serpentine maze of half-clad club patrons as they headed to Palladium, and they found themselves unable to speak over the club din, just grin and laugh, nodding at someone nearby dressed outrageously. At one point, Keldon reached out his hand, and Josh took it. Keldon felt happier than he could remember being in a long time.

Impossible as it was to believe, the music on the dance floor pumped louder, and they merged with the pulsating population, dancing where they could, moving in ways that would not harm those around them.

They danced.

Keldon felt a surprising surge in raw enthusiasm for dancing, for being in this club with a handsome man. He even thought well of Catherine Maggiarra at this moment, their patron saint of expensive sushi and limo rides. As he twisted and spun, he regularly glanced at Josh, watching him spin his own unique moves. They would catch each other's eye and nod a sexy *I see you* at each other, leering, grinning shyly, suggesting to each other with arched eyes, *Yeah. I might take you home.*

Keldon fought the crowd for drinks on two separate occasions, springing for doubles. They danced for almost an hour.

During their third dance break, they toasted with water and each took a generous slug. Josh laughed, looking around and yelling into Keldon's ear, "This is so not me. I can't believe I'm here."

Keldon raised his glass. "To being here."

They toasted and gulped again, eager to refuel and enjoy the dance floor again. They danced together a few times, slight entanglements, brushing against each other with the right pressure to convey lust and flirty intention. After their last interaction, Josh had unbuttoned another shirt button.

Another fifteen minutes later, Josh's final button was freed and his shirt dangled open. Keldon liked what he saw, a stomach without much hair, a thin, brown treasure trail. Josh's body was not sculpted, not perfect. He had a small gut. And while Josh would never be called stocky, he was plump around the edges, the way a man is when he's active but he loves beer and does not mind saying hello to a brownie now and then. Keldon liked it, that freedom to love food enough to show it on your body. He didn't consider himself a chubby-chaser by any means, but the extra thick looked good on Josh.

"Nice paunch," a girl said, yelling, and turned her back.

Josh shrugged it off and leaned over to Keldon and yelled, "She's jealous of your being here with me."

Josh laughed after he said that, but Keldon knew that the comment had made Josh self-conscious. Keldon had a long history of paying attention to subtle tells, especially about body image issues. Steven had never quite trusted that Keldon had found his body desirable, though he did in many ways. That trust ate at the relationship, and even Keldon could barely influence it.

But if the woman's comment unnerved Josh beyond his initial awkward laugh, he didn't show it. Josh danced with the same enthusiasm he had demonstrated the previous hour. He danced with his shirt open, letting himself swing and spin, seemingly unaffected. He appeared to be having a good time.

Keldon realized he was also having a great time and danced into Josh's arms close enough to communicate with his eyes, *I'm having a good time with you.*

They kissed.

The next person to comment was a shirtless, muscled man roughly fifteen minutes later. Music obliterated most of the conversation between Josh and his shirtless detractor so Keldon only heard the second half of the sentence. "…it off, porky."

Josh turned away, continued his unique moves, and ignored the muscled man who grabbed Josh's arm and spun him back. "You should button up. You're grossing everyone out."

Keldon noted the muscle god wore a white designer wife-beater tucked into his expensive jeans.

Josh looked back in alarm and anger and surprise, irritated by the intrusion. He jerked his arm free.

Keldon instinctively knew how to respond and had already pulled up his own tee to his midsection, drawing the gaze of the muscled, shirtless man, distracting him as he pulled the shirt over his head, soft puppy muscles lean and bouncy.

The muscle man responded with appreciation and pointed at Keldon. "This kid can take off his shirt. He's got abs people wanna see."

Keldon followed through with the second half of his plan and slid up against Josh instantly, and turned his head sharply to meet for a fat kiss. He sucked Josh's lower lip and felt Josh's body tremble; the two of them stopped moving their feet in a world of mad-leaping dancers. The moment, pure, radiant purple in Keldon's mind, lasted forever.

When they drew apart, the muscle man was gone. They hadn't noticed, still staring at each other, panting, feet not yet stampeding with the human cattle every inch around them. Instead, they stared and stared more, finally reminding their toes to move, remembering to hop and twist and slide, and they danced again, indistinguishable from any other patrons except for the big smiles on each of their faces, which they hid behind their arms, reaching, grasping, swaying over their heads.

They danced.

* * * *

They left the club a half-hour later, Josh promising he might die if he did not sleep almost immediately. Keldon dragged Josh through the club, holding his wet sweaty hand. They buttoned up and readied themselves for early May's bracing wind from nearby Lake Michigan. Keldon pulled out his cell phone to call the limo driver.

"Let's walk," Josh said. "It's not far."

"We're all sweaty. We'll get a cold or something."

"Maybe. Probably not. It's a crazy night for me. I wanna do something different."

Keldon smiled shyly. "What about making out shirtless in the back of a limo?"

Josh looked him in the eyes. "Limo it is."

Keldon loved the act of kissing, the sheer innocence of the act. Kissing expressed "I find you attractive" in a way words would always fail. Kissing could express dominance, submission, equality. It was a form of listening, intuiting, a way of sharing an experience, reliving a moment or an evening together, its passions and softness, and the soft parting from a bottom lip gently chewed thrilled Keldon in a way sex could never touch. A kiss was pure.

A kiss was about mutuality. *Do you like me the way that I like you? You do? Good. Let's kiss again.*

He loved the way Josh kissed, the firmness of his lips, the hunger in him. He loved the insistence for this intimacy and the way Josh caressed Keldon's face, fingers tracing along the jawline making Keldon feel desired. He loved feeling desired.

With the light traffic at the late hour, they arrived at the Drake too soon for both men. Keldon began recapping the night, explaining what a really great time he had.

"Stay the night," Josh said. "Not for sex. I don't really fool around before I know someone. And I'm not trying to sneakily suggest, 'Let's have morning sex because I'm super tired right now.' I'm saying, 'Spend the night. We'll sleep in our underwear and cuddle.'"

"I shouldn't do that," Keldon said. "I want to, trust me."

"Then, you should totally do this. Besides, maybe I talk in my sleep and you'll learn something to use against me. You can blackmail me into telling Irene what you want me to. C'mon. Stay."

It felt wrong to Keldon, but Josh wanted it and he wanted it too. He did want it, but did he want it because he wanted to squeeze Josh and hear him breathe quietly while asleep? Or did he want to further his agenda to get that serial killer's painting? Whenever he remembered the task before him, he felt disgusted with himself all over again. How could he have let himself forget the reason for their date? The dancing and kissing had erased his mission.

"I should go," Keldon said. "I don't want to cramp your style or whatever."

Josh refused to let him out of the limo. "Can you be okay with not having sex? I promise I won't try anything. I like you a lot and you're sexy, but that's not enough for me to get all slutty on a first date."

Keldon laughed when Josh wriggled his eyebrows. The limo idled in front of the hotel.

Keldon said, "I really like you, and honestly, I'd like to stay. But sometime in the next week, I'm going to have to visit Irene and ask her again to sell us her paintings. I will ask Mrs. Maggiarra if she will budge on revealing more details, but she's kinda weird. This secrecy thing is important for some reason. Won't it be uncomfortable when I show up at Irene's again? If we spend the night together?"

"I don't mind. Irene knows you'll be back." Josh opened his door and offered his hand for Keldon to take. "And who knows, she may decide on her own to sell. I don't think it's about the money for her, but maybe it is. You have to work that out with her. But for tonight, let's not be employees who work for these tough broads. Let's just be horny guys who got overly tired clubbing in Chicago and fell asleep together. I will totally buy you breakfast in the morning."

Keldon took Josh's hand and felt something like relief to have made a decision. "You know that if I spend the night, I'll end up paying for breakfast tomorrow on Mrs. Maggiarra's budget."

"I hope she'll reimburse you for organic eggs," Josh said.

Keldon tried not to grin and thanked the limo driver, tipping what he hoped was generous. He didn't want to be thought of as cheap.

They held hands as they walked to the front revolving entrance.

Once in the lobby, Josh said, "What's she like, Mrs. Maggiarra?"

As they walked toward the wood-paneled elevators, Keldon considered how much to reveal about her, an obviously private woman. He said, "She's very corporate-minded to me. She said she used to run a Human Resource department for this Mr. Mercer guy, and I think at her level it wasn't just hiring temps. I think she was involved in big deals and decisions, like close to a vice-president level. He agreed to let her use his name, and I would imagine his name means something to people in his industry. So there's a level of trust he has with her."

Josh said, "What's she like in person?"

"The same as I said just now. When I meet with her, I get the feeling I'm her employee getting talked down to because I went to a dentist outside the health insurance plan. I guess I don't know what exactly human resources does, but I think they're the people who yell at you if you didn't do your benefits right."

Josh said, "Yeah, basically. More than that but yeah, that kind of stuff. I worked for a big company for five years."

"Oh, where?"

"Just a place in New York. I mean, they were headquartered in Denver, but I worked at their New York corporate offices and then for another two years at their Madison office. So is she this crazy Italian lady or something, this Mrs. Maggiarra?"

Keldon laughed. "Hey, quit drilling me for information. I answered a Truth or Date question for you earlier, and you never took your turn. It's *my* turn to ask you stuff."

While teasing each other about who-owed-whom, the two men were reunited with the luxurious room. All they surveyed was sumptuous and supple. One french lamp on an exquisitely carved table in the far corner emitted a soft glow, tuck-in service welcoming visitors home. Keldon noticed small croissants and expensive chocolates on a silver platter sitting on the glass coffee table between the two couches. He touched Josh on the shoulder and nodded at the tray.

Josh smiled.

Keldon said, "Wanna drink?"

"Water," Josh said and then, "come check out this view. It's crazy."

Keldon strolled from the bar to find Josh's head touching the glass, the rest of him firmly balanced on his feet. Keldon found this endearing, this eagerness for the city, and nudged the bottled water against Josh's shoulder.

"Truth or Date." Josh accepted the bottle and unscrewed the cap. "Your turn to ask me."

"Okay," Keldon said. He took a long tug of water and said, "Truth or date?"

"Date," Josh said.

"How serious are you about this no-sex thing? Was that the truth or a ploy?"

"The truth," Josh said. "I try to slow things down. I dunno, maybe on the second date, but I think that given you and I have this other thing drawing us together, this crazy art deal, maybe not then either. Maybe we shouldn't fool around until this weird thing is settled. Assuming your client lady isn't ripping off Irene, we could see what's up after that."

Keldon was touched to hear that answer, frustrated, too. "Okay. Thanks."

"What about you?" Josh said, leaning closer to Keldon. "You okay with light kissing and shirts off and that's it? Would you have had sex with me tonight?"

"I don't know," Keldon said.

Josh laughed. "Cheater. I put my cards on the table."

"I really don't know," Keldon said. "Maybe. I like you. I think you're hot."

"You like my over-the-belt fat gut is what you like," Josh said with a grin that verged on laughter. "Thank you, by the way. That was one of the best date moments I've had with a guy in my life, so thank you for that."

Keldon blushed with pride, and they toasted water bottles, avoiding each other's eyes to scour the city view. Keldon wanted to remember it all, to savor the night.

"I don't date," Keldon said. "I can't afford to. Dating costs money, even if you're cooking home meals together. I don't have a budget for eating out or sometimes, you know, eating. At times I have limited myself to one meal a day for a few lean weeks. I don't have opportunities to have date sex. I might have gone through with it."

Josh nodded and looked into the city, double city, the reflected one in glass and the real one beyond glass, lighting the room with a thousand soft window glows. Keldon thought Josh looked amazing, the sparkle in his green shirt, the curve of his masculine shoulders, and his legs, thick and strong.

"Then again—" Keldon paused for emphasis. "—you accused me of having a big dick the first time I met you and told your boss I'd probably be no good in bed. So I've got that threat hanging over me. Maybe sex isn't a good idea."

"Hey." Josh's face creased in worry, and he stepped away from the window toward Keldon. "I'm really sorry about that. I was way out of line."

"I was kidding," Keldon said. "You apologized real nice, both you and Irene. I was teasing you."

Josh remained remorseful. "It was a dumb-ass thing to say, and I only said it because you are really handsome and I could tell you were not into me at all. It was kinda crushing me to have you look down on me that day. That's not an excuse. I was basically pretending to be Forrest Gump but with fewer catchphrases. I know I set you up. I just didn't know how much it would sting. So I was a dickhead to you. I'm sorry."

Keldon raised his arm and touched Josh's face. "It's okay. I was kidding."

Josh nodded and looked out the window. "I still feel bad about it."

"Don't," Keldon said and was surprised he truly meant it. That little joke and Josh's guilt represented good leverage for later influence, but Keldon didn't care. He found himself surprised that he really was letting go of being Mrs. Maggiarra's employee. He was Keldon on a date. A good date.

They kissed at the window, stopping to glance at the city, pointing out landmarks to each other. They mightsay, "What do you think that light is over there?" even though neither knew the answer. But it was fun to point out the night-shapes and distant light shows and speculate. It was a clear night, and they could see far.

Josh said, "Not to be too nosy, but do you really have so little money that you don't eat?"

"Some weeks. And I don't mind your asking. It is what it is."

"What about ramen noodles?"

Keldon made a face. "I'd rather not eat those. But I will. Doesn't make them less disgusting."

After a short silence, Josh said, "I will die if I don't sleep soon. I swear to you. Pioneer man isn't used to being up this late. My body wakes up at four thirty every morning. I'm gonna try to sleep in tomorrow, but I might not sleep past six. I've got to go to bed. But first, I call dibs on the shower. I'll be fast."

He grabbed a croissant on the way to the master bathroom.

Keldon watched him leave the room with the pleasure of remembering their night and knowing there was one more piece left, sleeping, and he smiled. *So this is dating. This is a date.*

He liked it.

* * * *

By the time Keldon finished his shower and crawled into bed, Josh was flung across the entire thing, facedown and spread-eagle as if recently murdered. Josh responded to gentle prodding, allowing himself to be corralled onto one side of the bed while Keldon made room for himself.

After a good-natured grumble and a rumbly, "You smell nice" from Josh's side, they maneuvered into spooningtaking pleasure in finding the right contact points on the crisp, expensive linens.

"Truth or date?" Josh said in a dreamy voice.

"Truth," Keldon said quietly.

"Do you think people are basically good or basically terrible?"

Keldon said, "Let me think about it."

Josh slurred his words. "After tonight, I think good."

Keldon didn't want to answer, not with the answer in his heart. Why ruin the evening? While debating the right words, he felt the rhythmic breathing next to him and came to realize Josh had fallen asleep, or was at least in that thin trance that precedes actual sleep. With very little motion, Keldon pulled Josh tighter and inhaled the smell of them together. He reveled in the wealth surrounding them in the four-poster bed, Josh's warm skin, the thousand yellow window squares still projecting light through their sitting room, light sneaking into the bedroom to remind them of the city's protective embrace.

With their bodies pressed together, Keldon could feel Josh slip deeper into sleep and thought to himself, *Some people are good.*

Chapter Five

Catherine Maggiarra stared at Keldon through her glasses and asked him again, "So, what progress?"

Keldon said, "They make those bifocals now where it's more integrated so you don't have to stare so hard over your glasses at a person. They're called progressives."

She didn't say anything. Keldon was amused anyway. It was his first attempt at levity with her, and for some reason, he didn't care if she thought it was funny.

"We had our date last Friday," Keldon said after another moment of silence. "I've been in contact with him twice since that night, and I visited Irene Woullet again yesterday. Josh was present. I spoke with Irene for roughly thirty minutes, but she's not willing to sell with the amount of information you're revealing."

"You offered her more money?"

"I did. I upped the offer just like you said, and she doesn't want it. I think the best bet might be to just tell her which painting we want. She's worried she's selling some masterpiece to an art thief and it will never get back to the right museum. Or maybe she's just being stubborn."

Catherine sat back in her chair. "Okay. Well, we tell her. But what do you think, Keldon? You're close to these people now, the nurse at least. Is she going to sell?"

"I honestly don't know. She ought to. This week on the phone, Josh confirmed her finances aren't good. He figured since you already knew, he wasn't doing a disservice by confirming it to me. He doesn't think this is about money. She just wants to know what's going on."

Mrs. Maggiarra pondered this.

Keldon said, "I've given this some thought, and I think there are two reasons she might sell it to you, but these only become valid after I tell her which painting you want and why."

Catherine perked up.

"First, Mrs. Woullet doesn't seem like the type to collect serial-killer art for its own value. She may not want it at all after she knows who painted it. She seems classy that way. Second, right now she thinks it was painted by her sister. She told me that on my first visit. Irene used to insist every family member or friend paint her something. She has a den full of these amateur paintings. Irene's going to be crushed to know that her sister didn't actually create it, but instead bought an unsigned painting at a garage sale and mailed it to her. She might want to get rid of it because of that disappointment with her sister. They were pretty close."

"Thank you for giving this some thought," Catherine said. "I have to admit that after seeing your expense report for your Chicago date, I began to wonder about your commitment. I thought maybe you were playing me for spending money."

"I'm sorry." Keldon turned bright red. "You said money was not a problem, and I assumed, oh god, I'm sorry—"

She held up her hand. "Apology rejected. I told you money was not a problem, and I meant it. But a limo from Wisconsin is a little more than I anticipated. But it's not the money."

Humiliation and shame raced through Keldon. He was almost at the verge of tears and sickness thinking of having to pay her back. Still, a small part of him thought defiantly, *It's always about the money.* He'd lucked into this ridiculous opportunity to make incredible money, and now he could be fired for ordering expensive sushi and a luxury limo. He cringed and awaited her next command.

Catherine said, "I understand you have two dates with the nurse. One still coming up."

"Yes," he said, blushing.

"And what's happening on that date?"

Keldon couldn't stop feeling small and humiliated. He could not let go of the money issue. He had really thought she meant it when she said, 'money was no object.'

He took a breath and tried to meet her gaze. "He's making me a pot roast at his house in Madison. I-I will need to rent a car for that."

"Good," she said, "that works out. I need you to get a rental car for Acquisition Number Six."

Keldon nodded and relief flooded through him. He wasn't fired. She had not mentioned him paying back the exorbitant date night. He looked down, eager not to meet her gaze.

"Keldon," she said, and his gaze snapped to her. "I meant what I said. It's not about the money. You're not in trouble. I was worried about your commitment. I know you don't know much about my story or why I'm collecting Merrick's art. And you're completely meeting my expectations, quite frankly. But when you turned in your expense report, I got nervous. I thought maybe you had lost track of what I need you to do."

"Okay." He found his gaze meeting hers more easily. "I get that. And I haven't lost track."

"I know." She nodded. "You've been thinking about how to get the painting. That's what I needed to hear. Spend what you need to spend. Do what you need to do. I don't want you to mislead this nurse. I don't intend to tell you how to conduct yourself on a date, but I don't want you to romance this painting out of the house. I have made clear there can be no deception or lies. Nothing illegal. Everything must be aboveboard. But this 'two dates' idea to persuade each other's agenda is just the kind of fast-thinking I had hoped for from you. I knew you would be resourceful. Keep at it. But Acquisition Number Five isn't full-time work, so I'd like to get started on the next one if you think you can split your focus."

Keldon relaxed and took another breath, bigger this time. "Yeah, that's fine. Let's talk about Number Six."

Mrs. Maggiarra looked through her glasses and opened the file in front of her. She lifted a piece of paper and frowned before saying, "Oh great. Another unicorn."

* * * *

Keldon found himself driving to Freeport, Illinois, close to the Wisconsin border. He focused the entire trip on his imminent responsibility: convincing a man in his sixties to sell a unicorn painting.

As Keldon approached his destination, he spotted the man he assumed was Frank Ahrens pacing the driveway. Keldon checked the time on the clock and saw he was on time, a few minutes early. The man was average height and had gray hair that stuck out on the sides, reminding Keldon somehow of duck feathers. The man wore an alarmed expression, as if Keldon were coming to take him to jail.

Keldon nodded, and the man walked out of the driveway, standing in front of the house. Keldon surveyed the house, looking for indicators that might help him proceed with this acquisition. The house was typical of its neighborhood, not completely abandoned but not exactly boasting home improvements either. The front porch sagged to the point of no return, jagged wooden planks sticking out at wrong angles. A dirty shadow against the house indicated where an awning once resided over the front door, and a similar shadow near the front window suggested a matching shutter had existed at one point. Tufts of spring emerged from the ragged brown and mildly green grass, weeds eager to get a jump start on the growing season. Something told Keldon if Frank Ahrens got the money, he wouldn't invest in lawn care.

Keldon hadn't even turned off the car engine when the man approached the driver's side window and said, "Do you have the money? Did you bring it?"

Keldon did not like Frank Ahrens' eagerness and debated getting out of the car. In the end, acquiring the painting was more important than his mild trepidation, so he decided to establish the tone for the remainder of their conversation. He did not answer Mr. Ahrens' question but rather unbuckled himself slowly and indicated with his head Mr. Ahrens should back away from the driver's side door so he could emerge.

Frank Ahrens hopped back a few feet and then walked briskly to his front porch, pulling open the cheap metal screen door to lock the sturdier inside door.

Having done so, he jogged down the front cement porch steps and said again, "Did you bring the money?"

Keldon stood next to the car in his charcoal-gray suit and adjusted the knot of his light blue tie. His tie required no adjustment. He just wanted Mr. Ahrens to note the suit, the professionalism, and defer to him.

"Do you have the painting?" Keldon said archly.

Frank Ahrens cocked his head. "Yeah. I have it."

Keldon didn't believe it but did not say anything. He knew how to draw the man out.

"Not here." Frank looked down and shifted his weight to the other foot. "It's in my storage unit. But I'm pretty sure it's there. I'm sure of it. We'll go there now."

Frank Ahrens quickly walked to the passenger side of the car and tugged on the handle, indicating Keldon should open it. Keldon found it odd that the two men hadn't introduced themselves, but he understood from Mr. Ahrens' perspective Keldon was nothing more than a lackey, "the money man" as Josh had once described him. Why bother wasting time getting to know the man holding the check when it was the *check* that was truly desired? Keldon understood Mr. Ahrens. It was about the money.

Once both men were seated and buckled up, Frank Ahrens again promised its location, the storage unit. He seemed agitated. Keldon did not share this agitation and he did not like it, the mumbled, jagged movements from the man in his passenger seat.

"It's there." Mr. Ahrens jerked forward in the seat. "It has to be."

The more the man protested his confidence in its location, the less assured Keldon felt. Today could be a wasted errand. However, if the painting truly was in the storage unit, Keldon had to acquire it. Frank Ahrens gave terse directions, speaking as if Keldon knew Freeport well.

"Mr. Ahrens, may I ask you a question?"

"Yeah, sure. You have the money, though, right?"

"I do. Why did you buy this particular painting?"

"I knew it would be worth money," Frank Ahrens said with a twinge of confidence. "And I was right. Besides, I didn't buy it. I traded it for four guns."

"Guns?"

"Yeah. It was a sweet trade because one of the guns didn't even work. I mean, I told him that, I told Jim the Colt don't work, but he didn't care. He wanted it anyway. He said he could fix it, but I think he'd be more likely to blast off his own head first. He don't know shit about guns. It was old."

"What made you decide to trade?"

"I thought it would be worth money." Frank Ahrens's glee was almost childlike. "And I was right. *Worth* it."

Keldon quelled his resistance to point out that based on the check he brought with him, clearly the painting wasn't worth that much.

"Right?" Frank said. "You brought the money?"

"Yes," Keldon said, growing weary of this topic. He wondered if he should worry about how often Frank asked for the money. He did not like the idea of heading to a deserted storage unit accompanied by a man who bartered with guns. On the other hand, Keldon didn't feel particularly threatened at this moment, just cautious and alert for more warning signs.

Keldon said, "Did it bother you to own a painting by a serial killer?"

"Huh? No. No, I didn't care. I thought it would be fun to show around, how I owned art by someone famous."

"Yes," Keldon said, unable to stop himself, "famous for *killing* people."

"So? I didn't kill nobody. I didn't do nothing wrong."

Keldon didn't particularly feel like arguing the ethics of the transaction, especially when he wasn't sure how he himself stood on the matter. Couldn't someone argue that he was just as ghoulish as Mr. Ahrens? Wasn't Keldon also collecting serial-killer art for money? He decided not to press the conversation further.

"They laughed at it," Frank said. "My friends saw it was a unicorn with a silver-green tail and green eyes, and they thought it was a joke. That I was kidding. Nobody believed it was painted by a celebrity."

Keldon didn't love thinking of Merrick as a celebrity, but he supposed he truly was. Mostly awful people were celebrities these days it seemed. No denying that.

The storage yard was easily visible from the highway, but that didn't stop Frank from pointing and saying, "There it is. Right there."

Keldon was surprised the lot was busy, which made him feel less vulnerable. The five or six other cars present on the premises made him happy. They drove up two aisles of mini-garages with orange corrugated doors until Frank remembered the right one. When they approached the correct unit, Frank opened his car door before Keldon fully stopped the car.

Frank paused with the door open. "You said you brought the check."

"I did."

"Can I see it?"

"When you show me the painting, I'll show you the check."

"This could take a while." Frank looked at the rows of storage doors, as if he had planned to search each one.

"I can wait."

"Aren't you going to help look?"

Keldon said, "No. I'm parking down there at the end of this row. When you have the painting, come back to the car. But you're on your own in there."

"Go faster if you helped."

Keldon shook his head. "Not a chance."

Keldon had no intentions of following this jerky, gun-trading man into his storage unit. Perhaps his job, the constant awareness of serial killers in the world, guided his decision.

Frank nodded grimly. He hopped out of the passenger side and fumbled with his rental unit keys. He walked toward the locked unit and didn't think to lean over and shut the car door. Keldon wasn't surprised. Frank Ahrens didn't seem like a man who thought much about others.

When Frank liberated the orange door and sent it flying up its rails, Keldon could see the enormous junk stacks: boxes, two abandoned window air-conditioner units, dusty filing cabinets, and a field hat that might have come from a park ranger. He could see a box of cassette tapes,. The unit was overwhelming chaos.

Frank examined the tall stacks and turned toward the car. He said, "This could take a while."

"You know where to find me." Keldon reached over to close the passenger door.

He backed his rental down the alley until he was perched right at the T intersection on the heavily populated side, in view of the office. As he watched Mr. Ahrens disappear into the garbage jungle inside the cement shed, Keldon was pleased he had uncovered a limit regarding what he would and would not do for money. That was nice, to know there were limits. And his experience with Irene and Josh convinced Keldon to make sure he paid greater attention, was even more careful about making assumptions.

Twice, Frank Ahrens hustled down the pavement, appearing at Keldon's window to say, "How much for this? Do you think your boss would like this?"

The second time, Frank presented a carved mask. "It's African," he explained.

"Nothing but the painting," Keldon said both times.

Frank Ahrens hustled up the concrete the same way he hustled down it and disappeared within the storage shed confines again. When Keldon saw Frank hustling toward him a third time, twenty minutes later, some mysterious package under his arm, Keldon groaned. He feared he would have to get stern with Mr. Ahrens, and he did not want to do so.

Instead, Frank Ahrens greedily presented the unicorn painting and said with a flourish, "Ta-da!"

After returning a much happier Frank Ahrens to his decrepit home, Keldon locked the painting in his briefcase and put the horror in the trunk. It was the first time he had put the briefcase in the trunk, and he discovered he liked the sensation of being more physically distant from the art. He sensed a ritual forming at that moment, locking the art in the trunk after each filthy acquisition.

Full of the day's triumphs, he called Josh's house to hear his voice and feel pleasant for a few moments.

He was mildly surprised when Josh answered the phone.

"Hey, Chicago," Josh said.

"Hey there, Jebediah," Keldon said. "It's almost noon. I assumed you'd be out plowing fields by now or collecting rainwater."

"Yes, my life is hilarious, I know." Josh laughed.

Keldon suddenly felt sour, like he had overteased him but had not meant to push so hard in that direction. He tried to make up for it right away. "Seriously, what are you doing today? Nurse day? Day off?"

"Day off. And you guessed right, it's a farming day. There are four of us who share a decent-sized garden plot each year. We're not planting yet, but getting everything ready. Unpacking winter stuff, cleaning the area, digging. Adding in some natural fertilizers. It's a good afternoon's work for the four of us."

"Feel like getting some dinner after all that hard work?" Keldon said. "I'm in Freeport and could swing up your way. Not Mrs. Maggiarra's dime. My very own treat."

"That sounds nice," Josh said. "But I gotta pass. We have to complete this garden stuff today, and I don't know what time we'll finish. It's a pretty big patch. By the time we're done, it'll be getting dark, which means I won't have much time before bed."

"Seriously? The sun sets at almost 9:00 p.m."

"Actually, it's projected for 8:02 p.m. If I work until seven or seven thirty, that's not much daylight remaining. I don't always go to bed at sunset... I often stay up later than that, but I need to make dinner and get stuff ready for tomorrow. I have a lot more household chores that have to be finished by sunset. This is why guys don't date me. I told you."

Keldon said, "Okay, no problem. I was being spontaneous. I didn't know I'd be free this early. I thought I might be digging through a storage shed all day or some guy's basement. I feel like playing hooky."

Keldon had lied. It *was* a problem. It irritated him. A quick dinner wasn't asking much.

"Hooky, huh? More art?" Josh asked.

Keldon felt very self-conscious all of a sudden, feeling he had somehow said too much. But in a slow voice, he said, "Yes."

"We still on for this weekend?" Josh veered them out of strange and uncomfortable territory. "You still game for our Saturday date?"

"Yup." Keldon felt the gladness return. Saturday was something to look forward to.

"Good. You're the reason I have to work all day in the garden. We were supposed to do it this Saturday, but I got them to reschedule for today, so it's your fault I'm off to do hard manual labor."

Keldon felt a startling pleasure in hearing that, knowing he was worth changing plans to free up Saturday. To mask this pleasure from Josh, he teased him, saying, "I feel terrible. Really, I do. So, Saturday you said we'd start early?"

"Yeah, I was thinking around 7:00 a.m. If you want, Friday night you can crash at my place or get a hotel room. Either way. But we're going somewhere that opens early."

"And you won't say what?"

"I will not. Saturday is my date all day. Mystery date."

"Okay, then. See you Saturday morning. I'll get a hotel. If we're going somewhere that early, I need to sleep well the night before. Mrs. Maggiarra will totally pay for that. But the bigger question is, who dates in the *morning*, for god's sakes."

"Really," Josh said in a droll voice. "Who *does* that?"

Keldon laughed. "See you Saturday."

They teased each other a moment longer, delaying the good-bye until Keldon finally hung up, smiled, and drove the serial-killer art straight to Catherine Maggiarra.

Chapter Six

Keldon woke up at 6:00 a.m. Saturday morning and smiled with satisfaction. He liked waking up in fancy hotels. In more rigorous travel guides, the Madison Concourse hotel might only pass as a high-end three-star hotel, but in Madison, the Concourse was plenty fancy for four stars. The linens were a higher thread count, the bathroom boasted red marble with polished silver faucets, and the bed was clustered with a dozen exotic, decorative pillows. Keldon liked it. He liked expensive things, no denying that. He liked the silver-striped fabric wallpaper in the Concourse, the thin, fuzzy texture under his fingertips when he ran his finger against the wallpaper grain. He enjoyed disheveling both wrinkle-free king-sized beds. The night prior, he had used one bed for watching television and enjoying room service, the other for sleeping.

Not counting the impromptu sleepover at the Drake hotel, more than a year and a half had passed since Keldon had spent the night in an upscale hotel. Keldon reflected on his favorite hotel, the one he and Steven had rented for a month in Belize with the breakfast balcony overlooking the Caribbean Sea. Keldon caught himself, the error in his remembering, 'he and Steven rented.' *Steven* had rented. It was one of the ways he fooled himself, pretending *we* paid for things when it was only Steven. He had sometimes gotten lost in the *we*, the fiction that they were equal and wanted the same things. When Steven felt restless and wanted to fly somewhere for the weekend, Keldon felt he must want the same thing.

Some of that confusion lingered, that inability to separate *we* from *me*.

Padding naked across the Concourse's birthday-cake-colored carpeting, Keldon fumbled his way into the expansive bathroom, as large as his living room in his Chicago apartment. He smiled at the calming beige-and-peach interior, the glassy red marble, and solid glass shower door trimmed in gold. He didn't have to worry about the water bill so he would take his time this morning standing under the spray.

Aamir always evaluated the true sophistication of the hotel based on the quality of their soaps and shampoo, so Keldon did as well. The Concourse offered organics, private label. Aamir would have turned up his nose, but Keldon was suitably impressed.

As he opened the french rosemary-cream soap and passed it under his nose, Keldon remembered the night in the Drake hotel. Josh had asked him if he wanted sex. Keldon didn't know. Why didn't he know? Why couldn't he tell if he wanted sex? Keldon had decided he didn't have enough practice knowing what to want in a dating situation. Whoever paid the bills got to want things. The other team did not.

As the hot water bounced off the planes of his naked back, pounding its way down to the soft curve of his ass, he wondered again why he couldn't tell if he wanted sex. How could it be possible to not know? He let the water berate him, pound against his forehead and face while roving steam rose from beneath him, curling around his legs and snaking up his thighs.

He thought about Josh, the thickness of him, holding him from behind while in bed. How they kissed in the morning, an awful-morning-breath kiss. No romanticizing it, neither one of them tasted great. Keldon had never let himself kiss Steven or Aamir with morning breath. The very act of kissing without preparation was shocking, but Josh had grabbed him. Keldon did not resist. They'd kissed and hugged, Josh's chest and his thick arms squeezing him. He remembered the weight of Josh's arms, working-class arms.

Keldon looked down and saw his cock standing straight and proud, getting hammered with water. He thought to himself, *Well, that counts as an answer.*

With minimum guilt, Keldon skipped his morning workout routine. In preparation for the date, Josh told him to bring several changes of clothes, including clothes he could sweat in. He assumed a bike ride or long walk. That would count as the day's aerobics.

After mostly drying in the thick peach towels, he wrapped himself in the fluffy white robe the Concourse had provided and collapsed on his sleeping bed once more. Josh promised to meet him right in front of the Concourse hotel at 7:00 a.m. He still had a half hour. He decided to lie naked on the bed and watch television, the most decadent thing he could think to do in the last half-hour.

* * * *

Keldon emerged from the sliding glass doors at 6:55 a.m. to find Josh already waiting, sitting on the pavement with his back to the brick façade.

"Good morning," Keldon said, surprised. He was used to being the one who showed up early.

"Morning," Josh said, rising. "Hey, can we check your overnight bag with the concierge for an hour or so? You may not want to carry it around. I mean, you *can*. No biggie."

The two men faced each other briefly before heading back to the concierge, and for a moment, Keldon didn't know if they would kiss hello or not. But he now *knew* he wanted to kiss Josh, and that self-awareness made him smile.

In front of the Concierge desk, Keldon leaned in. "Good morning."

Josh smiled. "Good morning."

They kissed.

After Keldon stuffed the claim check in his front pocket, Josh ushered them out the front door with a hand at the small of Keldon's back and, once on the sidewalk, turned Keldon in the desired direction, toward the state capitol.

The Wisconsin air was sharp and cool, like spring was having second thoughts about extending its visit, but the green on trees already proved too lush for a retraction. The spring beginnings Keldon had witnessed in the Turners' small town had finally revealed their green secrets. Spring had sprung. The leaves did not boast summer's emerald-green thickness, but rather dressed a lime-green sleeve down each branch, ready to expand farther with each additionally sunny day.

"I saw the state capitol last night," Keldon said as the massive structure loomed before them. "The dome was all lit up. Really beautiful."

"Yeah," Josh said. "They give tours inside all summer. It's amazing."

Josh explained the massive dome was dwarfed only by Washington, DC's more famous construction, and Keldon believed it. The dome dominated all of the morning sky and even a chunk of landscape. The capitol itself struck Keldon less as an achievement in engineering and more of a cake baker's dream: a bone-white-frosted wedding cake, layer upon layer of carefully sculpted icing. The dome boasted proud columns under its creamy base, exaggerated bunting circling its construction. At the very tip-top of the dome, to Keldon's delight, was a cake topper.

"It looks like a giant cake," Keldon said, nudging Josh.

Josh glanced at the capitol. "I'd eat it."

Keldon needled Josh for details, trying to drag out clues.

Josh said, "Keep your pants on. We're literally less than two minutes away. It's really not that big a deal. I'm sorry I made it seem more exciting than it really is."

They crossed the street to the capitol, and Keldon looked around, admiring the blooming branches, the pink buds opening on a nearby crab apple tree, framed against the shining white dome that always stayed in the background. A surprising number of people already strolled the area, entering or leaving breakfast cafes or just meandering around the square. Keldon found the scene beautiful. Inspiring, even. He was happy to be here.

"Here we are," Josh said after they had gone not much farther. In fact, they hadn't even walked a full side of the capitol. There was nothing Keldon would have called *here* except for three dozen card tables, hastily arranged as if they had gotten up too early to make themselves presentable.

Keldon looked around the casual assembly and read the green banner dangling between two trees. He read it aloud. "Farmers' Market."

With excitement, Josh said, "Wait until you see this place in June and July. It's crazy. Only hardcore merchants show up in May. Some of these places here today have hydroponic vegetables for sale or sell year-round stuff."

"Looks like jams, honey," Keldon said, "cheeses."

"Yeah. Some good early spring crops but not too much of everything, which is why you have to get here early. I try to base my life on eating quality local stuff. Might get some good chard today."

"Or extra-crispy fried chicken," Keldon said.

Josh chuckled.

Keldon wasn't convinced it was worth the early wake-up to arrive for these scattered goods, but he kept his judgment to himself and followed Josh from table to table as he greeted merchants with enthusiasm. Some merchants recognized Josh, even if they didn't know him by name. He was a friendly face, a regular customer.

"Best goat cheese," Josh said to Keldon while making his purchase. "Seriously. If you like goat cheese, you should buy some."

Keldon nodded but did not. Goat cheese was a delicacy he would have no use for. His home-cooked meals were meager affairs. He relied heavily on cheap spices to add exotic flavors to bland foods. Only since he started working for Mrs. Maggiarra had he begun to trust food to remain in his pantry until the next influx of funding. He had already begun replenishing staples: bags of noodles, canned soups for future lean times. Cheese was still a luxury.

Josh made purchases, some surprising Keldon, like a homemade taupe shirt made of a durable fabric.

Keldon rubbed it between his fingers, curious. "What is this?"

"It's a chambray. Less processed than what we're used to in a department store, which means it lasts longer. Wrinkle-resistant because of how she makes it. But light, airy. Summer shirt. Rub it against your skin."

Keldon agreed the texture felt creamy. But this only strengthened his desire to feel Josh against his skin.

Josh said to the vendor, "I lost your email address over winter, so I couldn't contact you about a special order. I'd like another one just like this in light blue. One white with shorter sleeves. Can we set that up?"

Once his shirt-ordering was complete, it didn't take long to explore the entire market. Josh chatted with regulars about the previous winter since this was the first appearance for the summer run. They talked about spring rain and its influence on early broccoli. Josh told his winter stories, and his merchant friends told theirs. A new customer's presence would end the quick catch-up, and they would part as friends who still hadn't learned each other's names. Keldon found the whole thing convivial. Charming, even.

With Josh's purchases tucked into bicycle knapsacks, now belted about his waist, they strolled away from the market, continuing their walk around the capitol square. Keldon was surprised yet again at the active morning pedestrian traffic. He had assumed Madison would be sleepy on a Saturday morning. He changed his assumption.

The sun projected a little more confidence in its innate abilities, and Keldon soon felt warmer. He looked up to see the blue sky with white wisps through the exploding green on tree branches everywhere.

"I love the farmers' market," Josh said. "Over the summer you get to form these relationships with farmers and talk about their bees and their organic solutions for growing the best vegetables. It's fascinating. We're all going to have to live this way again when the economy collapses, eating locally and growing everything we can. I love that people are already embracing this, not out of fear, but because they want it."

Keldon thought Josh sounded happy.

"Kind of a grim outlook for the future." Keldon wondered privately how much to read into Josh's pessimistic prediction.

"Just saying. There's some finance podcasts I listen to that are pretty dark. Peak oil, reliance on fossil fuels, climate change. The world is failing. We have to get ready."

Keldon didn't want to dig too deep, not yet. He could let the doomsday predictions slide for now.

"I couldn't help but notice there was no KFC table," Keldon said.

"Shut up," Josh said cheerfully. "Don't ruin this beautiful morning by pointing out I'm a hypocrite."

Josh guided them toward a small business fitted at the tip of a triangular block, an eatery with big, bouncy letters plastered on their floor-to-ceiling windows offering promises such as DELICIOUS! and NOW SERVING BREAKFAST! Josh pointed at the tiny restaurant's name, Teddywedgers, as their destination.

"They've been at this same location for thirty years," Josh said. "It's a culinary institution in Madison. I often stop here after the farmers' market."

Keldon was not impressed. "It looks like a late-night dive where they warm up cold pizza under a heat lamp."

"It's not that bad. Besides, you have to eat here with me. Today's *my* date."

Keldon grumbled but was secretly pleased Josh wanted to show him favorite spots. He didn't know why this delighted him, but it did. Perhaps it meant the date mattered.

Josh gushed about the beef-filled Cornish pasty until Keldon finally agreed to try one, but Josh said they weren't available until after 11:00 a.m. He only wanted to explain just how good they were. Keldon rolled his eyes. They both ordered breakfast pies, bacon and eggs, and Keldon was surprised when their aluminum-wrapped breakfasts weighed down his hand. The thing felt like a solid pound.

Josh led him back to the courthouse square, to a grassy bank where he plopped into the grass. They unwrapped the heavy breakfast pies and toasted as they might champagne.

"Check out the tulips," Josh said, pointing. "In a week, this entire area is going to be blasted with them. Look at all the ones getting ready to burst."

Keldon could see the hundreds of green stalks bob silently in the morning breeze, the threat of imminent explosion easy to ignore until your eye recognized the sheer quantity of them. Already, two or three dozen tulips emerged, an impressive quantity in anyone's lawn, but on the capitol's front yard, the final burst promised to be significant. Against the sculpted state capitol, the yellow-and-orange-streaked tulips looked almost noble, giving Keldon the impression of ordinary citizens who stood proudly for their government. Well, maybe not lately. Wisconsin had had its political troubles in the past year.

They chewed their breakfast pies, the warm eggs, cheese, and bacon inside a dry pocket of thick crust.

"This is terrible," Keldon said, munching.

"Yeah," Josh said, tearing off another bite.

Keldon said, "The eggs and cheese are good, but this crust is awful. It's incredibly dry and makes my tongue parch up."

Josh finished chewing and said, "Yeah."

"Why are we eating these again?"

Josh took another bite. "It's a culinary institution in Madison. Thirty years."

Keldon chuckled. "These crusts must have been part of the original batch."

They munched and watched the city hustle around them. The early-rising tulips bobbed *yes* in the spring breeze, as if agreeing summer should be allowed to visit.

After eating all of the bacon and egg filler, Keldon continued to munch on the remains of the crust, causing Josh to raise his eyebrows.

Keldon laughed. "It kinda grows on you. The taste."

After retrieving Keldon's overnight bag from the hotel, the two men strolled to Keldon's rental car and loaded Josh's bike. Josh provided directions through downtown's maze of one-way streets. Keldon hadn't paid much attention to neighborhoods on his arrival the previous night, so he was surprised to enter residential neighborhoods a mere three blocks from the state capitol. Starting the day downtown, Keldon had allowed himself to forget that Madison was merely a biggish small Midwestern town. Or a small big town. One of those. They stopped at a butcher to pick up the evening's roast, a prime selection from the Black Earth Meats, which Josh assured Keldon would taste unlike any other beef. They stopped at the Willy Street Co-op for that night's essential vegetables, those unavailable at the farmers' market. Josh asked Keldon his opinion on various side dishes and seemed pleasantly surprised to find Keldon well-versed in taste combinations.

Keldon picked up some shallots. "Maybe these to balance out the horseradish. Shallots mellow out sharpness but don't erase it."

Josh smiled. "Yeah. Good idea. What do you think about this morning's kale for tonight's salad?"

Keldon paused and considered going along with Josh's suggestion. But instead, what came out of his mouth were the words, "How about spinach?"

It was a small victory, if it could even be called a victory, but Keldon was aware of how different the experience was for him. On a date, he had allowed himself to disagree. To have an opinion.

"No problem," Josh said. "I love spinach too."

With access to a car, Josh shyly requested running a few errands for purchasing items he'd have difficulty transporting. They picked up a stack of library books from the main branch, thick mosquito netting that looked cumbersome to carry by bike, and a few heavy tools from a hardware store. Keldon was happy to oblige. In return, Josh narrated Madison's attractions by neighborhood, explaining the town's history he knew by heart. Keldon was surprised to find himself quite interested, surprised by the appeal.

"Did you know Frank Lloyd Wright grew up in Madison?"

"No," Keldon said. "I did not."

"A couple buildings he designed are around here."

"Maybe we can go check them out," Keldon suggested.

"Let's save that for another date. I have big plans for us this afternoon."

"Another date, huh?" Keldon smiled.

Josh laughed and blushed but said no more.

Josh's house was one and a half stories, faded blue. The wrought iron railings had been painted to match the original siding, robin's egg blue. Although Keldon hadn't held any specific expectations about Josh's house, he was still surprised to see it blend into the neighborhood in a nondescript way. It simply didn't stand out as the "Pioneer House." The grass grew green, same as everyone else's, the promise of spring taking root everywhere around him. A few neighbors had already planted their spring flowers, while at that moment, Keldon observed other neighbors manicuring their yards this brisk Saturday morning, beginning their summer plantings.

As they walked up the front steps, a mysterious voice yelled, "They out yet?"

Keldon glanced around but couldn't trace the voice. He decided it was a neighbor yelling through her window.

Josh yelled his reply. "No, Mrs. Hemmer, not yet. A few dozen are blooming, but not the big show. They're almost ready."

"I might not go. I've seen them before," the voice answered in a loud, surly tenor.

"I'll take the bus with you, Mrs. Hemmer. We'll see them together."

This apparently did not warrant a response.

Josh turned to Keldon and murmured, "State capitol tulips. They're a big deal to everyone who lives here. You take your kids to see them, your elderly parents. It's like the fourth of July, and I'm not trying to be snarky. It's really impressive."

Though he had never been overly fond of tulips, per se, Keldon thought they fit the character of the capitol building itself, and the small detail made a good impression on him. Keldon noted with surprise that the serial-killer painting had not emerged once as a topic of conversation. No Truth or Date, just chatting, small preferences and amusing anecdotes along the lines of "This one time I saw…" Keldon liked it, this opposite feeling of their Chicago date. This intimacy, this shallot-purchasing intimacy was somehow more authentic, more earthy than even rubbing naked bellies at the former Excalibur nightclub, their shirts wide open. Keldon smiled at that memory, but he found this newly discovered "Farmers' market intimacy" even more alluring.

Aamir and Steven had created intimacy through wealth. Josh created it through the ordinary.

Keldon felt an odd twinge in each of the other rooms as they made trips to the car and unloaded Josh's items. Something was missing. He couldn't name it. The dining room had a sturdy table, a rough table, nothing polished and refined. The curtains were muslin crepe, stylish and slinky, not designed to keep light out but only prying eyes. Keldon looked around. With the meat and fresh vegetables in tow, Josh led them straight to the kitchen. It was here that Keldon looked around and finally realized what was missing. Everything.

Keldon said, "You don't have any pictures. No art or posters or anything."

"I'm pretty minimal." Josh indicated where Keldon should set the groceries. "I keep my photos in a scrapbook."

The cheery yellow kitchen was packed with useful necessities, a hand-powered juicer, herb plants on windowsills and ceramic bowls in every color of the rainbow. Keldon caught Josh's eyes and arched his eyebrows as he nodded at the rainbow bowls.

Josh said, "They're from my sister. I like them."

"Where's your butter churn, Jebediah?"

"That's where I draw the line," Josh said. "No churning butter. Grand tour?"

Keldon nodded, eager to see how Josh lived.

The other rooms' walls were as bare as the dining room. The living room boasted a mission-style sofa, a large wooden chest, and lamps on long silver poles. Keldon noticed books in every room, on the couch, an open one on the dining room table, and a beekeeper's hat on a peg near the front door.

Keldon said, "Bees?"

"Yeah, this summer I'm apprenticing with this couple that keeps bees on their property. They're going to teach me how. I met them through craigslist."

Because there were so few personal items scattered around the house, Keldon found it difficult to compliment Josh's home. He asked about the pile of knitting on the far end of the couch and the function of two enormous pipe-like structures leaning against the hallway leading to the bathroom.

"I'm not sure how I'll use those." Josh said, running his hand along one of the pipes. "I salvaged them. Maybe part of a garden watering thing. Dunno yet. You should have seen this house a year ago. I got in the habit of storing salvage finds in the house. Every room was packed with things I had the intention to use 'someday.' Ha. What a joke that was. I really had to binge clean at one point."

"Where'd you find this house?" Keldon asked. "Newspaper ad or craigslist or something?"

"A client of mine died here." Josh led them back to the kitchen. "I rent from his two kids. Let's get started on that pot roast."

"Wait, *died* here?"

"A lot of my patients die," Josh said, unpacking the potatoes and carrots. "I work with people who are dying or have progressive long-term illnesses. When the guy who lived here was close to death, his daughter asked me to recommend realty agents in town. She and her brother wanted to rent out their father's house for a year or two until they decided what to do with it, and voila, here I am three years later living in Mr. Ferguson's house. His name was Harry Ferguson."

Keldon marveled at how easily Josh told the story of living in a dead man's home.

"So his children…?"

"They still haven't decided what to do with the house. But they like me renting it, so for now, their decision is on hold. I like the cheap rent and having a whole house to myself. They like having a rental property with a tenant who isn't making problems."

"Most of your patients are terminal?"

"Not all but most, yes."

"That doesn't bother you? Being around so much death?"

"Death is natural. It's part of our life experience. We're all going to do it, so why get so freaked out about it? Besides, people are more honest when they're dying. When they're truly vulnerable. It's refreshing to skip over the bullshit of life."

Keldon tried to take this in, this casualness about death. He hadn't fretted over his own personal demise. He was much more invested in the problem of trying to stay alive. It surprised him how death was merely a coworker for Josh. He wanted to know more.

Josh assigned Keldon the task of washing the potatoes and cutting them into chunks while Josh chopped onions, shallots, and carrots.

Keldon said, "What about Mrs. Woullet? Is she more honest about stuff?"

"Absolutely. She'd never be friends with me if she were healthy. She and her husband weren't mega-rich, but they were rich enough. They had some bones. Had a summer cabin near Eau Claire. Do you think she'd hang out with the beekeeping nurse as her buddy? We'd never run in the same circles. But she's cut through all the bullshit. Her eyes are open. Dying does that to you."

"So she really is dying?"

"We all are," Josh said, "But yeah, her illness is progressing more rapidly now. She's only had nurses for the last year or so. That first day you stopped by? You caught her on a good day. She's starting to lose upper body function. Her arms don't work sometimes. She's terrified. She doesn't want to have someone feed her. People with muscular dystrophy can lose their ability to chew so they end up being intravenously fed for the last weeks or even months of life. It's not a great way to go."

Keldon hadn't considered Irene Woullet's death, not in any meaningful way. She looked healthy enough sitting amidst her books, tricking him into thinking she and Josh didn't get along.

"I'm sorry about Irene," Keldon said, not knowing how to express the confused admiration he felt for Josh or maybe for Irene's necessary courage.

"Me too." Josh grimaced. "It's hard for her. She was used to being independent. She's not looking forward to what's ahead."

Keldon looked through the kitchen windows to the backyard, rows of dirt already overturned, most likely for gardening. Keldon was mildly surprised that in addition to the patch of earth used for his garden, half the backyard was also torn up. In fact, the whole back yard was a wreck, he could see that from the window. A wire bird cage sat on a white picnic table, one recognizable structure among a dozen mysterious shapes. Clearly, these were more salvaged junk items dragged from Josh's home that served no clear purpose, not yet. The yard was full of mismatching items, metal contraptions, and wooden window frames, ready to be called into service. Items leaned against the garage, and a few were visible on the other side of the maple.

"Why wouldn't you and Irene be friends?" Keldon asked shyly. "You said she wouldn't be friends with you if she was healthy?"

"I didn't mean it quite like that," Josh said, pausing. "I didn't mean she *wouldn't* be friends with me. She wouldn't look at me and stick her nose up. She's cool. But how would we have ever met? Irene was corporate garden parties and charity events. She and her husband both worked big careers. Because of her illness, our lives intersected in a meaningful way, and when she leaves, I'll miss her. But it's so random to connect with someone who feels like your long-lost older sister and the circumstances of meeting are that she needs assistance dying."

Keldon considered that and thought about their date. Would they ever have enjoyed each other's company if not for these unusual circumstances? The two dates? That line of pondering made Keldon remember he hadn't done anything this morning to advance the cause, to soften Josh. On their Chicago date, Keldon thought about it a lot—what to do or say to win Josh over. Here in Madison, he hadn't been scheming. The realization surprised him. Although he felt mild guilt, the realization also pleased him.

Josh explained the evening's menu, the succulent pot roast with twelve distinct herbs simmering in its warm juices, the spinach salad with goat cheese, and Josh opened the fridge to reveal the lemon scones batter he assembled before biking downtown to meet Keldon. He explained that he'd bake them after dinner so they could eat them warm.

"I made a blueberry crème sauce from some of last summer's blueberries. I thawed them out last night. You drizzle it over the warm scones. There's a pinch of mint mixed in, which is hard to taste when you're eating it, but the frosting somehow tastes fresher."

Keldon was astonished. "You mixed all this before meeting me at the hotel this morning?"

Josh shrugged. "I get up early."

They finished chopping vegetables and necessary spices as the conversation morphed into a comparison of eating habits, what they cooked well, what they cooked when they were short on money, the cheapest meals they knew. Josh asked about Keldon's best meals, the best in his life, and Keldon described eating at a favorite French restaurant in Paris and lobster risotto in Florence. He worried for a moment he sounded pretentious, but while assembling their dinner in the crock pot, Josh elaborated on his favorite steak in New York City and spared no details in describing its virtues.

It struck Keldon as hard to reconcile, listening to Josh lustily describe another meal, the most tender lamb he ever tasted with the man who preferred not to use electricity in the evening.

"How do you live in winter without electricity or lights on?"

"I use electricity, even in the summer. I sometimes read at night if I'm feeling restless. For me it's like candy. I love it. I indulge. But I try not to gorge myself on it. I like living attuned to the rising sun. But I use heat and the gas stove, and I discovered a terrible and wonderful website called reddit. Have you heard of this? Well, apparently the whole world has. I'm late to the game. It's easy for me to lose hours on that site, so I try not to spend too much time on the computer. But my employer schedules my client time online and I read tons of articles about farming. Also, web-surfing for gay porn may disqualify me as a true pioneer."

"No, no," Keldon said, "you still qualify. They surfed for porn."

It comforted Keldon Josh wasn't as cutoff from civilization as he first seemed. Though the lack of paintings or personal touches in the home was somehow significant. Keldon hadn't formed an assumption as to what that meant, but it meant something. Josh had not mentioned his Madison friends or hanging out with friends, so perhaps he didn't entertain much in his home. The thought did not bother Keldon because wasn't he the same?

Keldon lived in a giant metropolis, but who were his friends? How often did he socialize? Poverty had a way of diminishing your social opportunities.

"What do you say to a bike ride?" Josh said. "I know a park where I think we should eat lunch. It's only a mile from here."

Keldon indicated he'd like to change clothes, and Josh suggested the downstairs guest room. "I won't come in. Plus, I've already seen you in your underwear, so no need to be shy."

After Keldon emerged ready to ride, he discovered Josh had not been idle. He had packed their luncheon feast in his bicycle knapsacks and led the two bicycles to the front of his house. Five minutes later, Keldon stared at Josh's butt once again, Josh leading the way as they pedaled through neighborhoods toward a park destination unknown. The houses whizzed by Keldon, and he found himself smiling.

Madison was not what he had expected. He had visited twice before, visits to Irene Woullet, but the trips had been business and his mind occupied with the acquisition. He generally didn't like being away from Chicago, needed the familiar thrum of thousands surrounding him to feel relaxed. But Madison evoked that same relaxed quality, which he found confusing. He didn't normally think of himself as a go-for-a-bike-ride type person, but as colorful bungalows and Cape Cods zoomed past, and the burgeoning shade of a thousand trees sheltered him, Keldon wondered how a town this welcoming and minty-fresh felt so much like coming home. He decided it was not the city, but his host.

"Not much farther," Josh yelled over his shoulder.

"You said that ten blocks ago," Keldon yelled back.

Josh laughed and grinned over his shoulder. "Not much farther."

But Keldon didn't mind. He really didn't.

Josh hadn't lied. Within two minutes they arrived at their destination, the Olbrich Botanical Gardens. Josh allowed his bike to coast to a stop, hopping to the ground as the wheels slowed enough to see the spokes once again. Keldon followed, walking his bike beside Josh as he led them through a brick-paved colonnade, a mission-style arbor affixed to paving stone columns every twelve feet. Already the brown, twisting vines bloomed early greens, not dominating the landscape, but it was obvious they soon would be restored to last summer's glory.

"We should have had this date next month," Josh said. "Everything would be greener and more lush. More impressive."

"Oh trust me," Keldon said, smiling. "I'm already impressed."

Josh laughed, pleased with the reply. "Virginia creeper vines do it for ya, huh?"

"You made a creamy blueberry drizzle at 5:00 a.m. I'm impressed."

Josh explained how he volunteered at the botanical gardens in the summers, helping maintain flowers and occasionally participating in heavy-lifting jobs, moving shrubs or clearing dead wood. He pointed to different flower beds and revealed what would soon appear in various spots. Keldon tried to envision the future life but couldn't, and although he felt too shy to say the words, he hoped he could come back again and see the gardens in a month or two when they bloomed full-strength.

Josh walked them to a gold-colored, gilded structure, a pavilion illustrating complex patterns of design, the pointy gabled roofs and intricate ornamentation screaming Thailand.

"This looks Thai," Keldon said. "It's like a Buddhist temple."

"Yeah. It was a gift from the government of Thailand to the U. The University of Madison has one of the largest Thai student populations outside Thailand. It's gorgeous, isn't it? I love it here."

Keldon agreed. The gold-leaf edges, rhythmic patterns, and attention to detail in every corner, every overhanging soffit, delighted Keldon's sense of order and harmony. He waltzed under it, looking up, humming while Josh unpacked their lunch on a nearby bench next to a koi pond. Except for a few couples strolling the grounds, they had the Thai pavilion to themselves. A private luncheon.

Josh enticed Keldon to his side with a soft whistle and indicated the meager spread on white linen. Keldon smiled and walked closer, feeling drunk. Drunk on the Madison sunlight, the beauty in intricately designed architecture, the generosity of foreign governments, on his enjoyment of a date where he was not pushing any agenda. As he walked closer, seeing bashful pride on Josh's face while fiddling with their lunch arrangements, Keldon experienced fleeting guilt at not executing Mrs. Maggiarra's wishes more faithfully in the moment, but he allowed that guilt to flit away like a butterfly he saw earlier.

"Okay," Josh said as Keldon joined him. "I made avocado and tomato sandwiches with a thin slice of turkey breast, homemade couscous with scallions, and pear slices. I didn't know how healthy you wanted to eat, so I also brought some ranch-flavored Doritos." He produced the small bag from behind the bench leg like magic, and Keldon laughed. He couldn't imagine a better luncheon.

"And I might eat a few," Josh said, pretending as if the outcome were uncertain. "There's lemonade in the thermos. We have to share a cup."

Keldon remained silent but allowed his face to beam his absolute delight.

The sandwich was one of the best things he had put in his mouth in weeks, and when he asked after the unique combination of flavors, Josh explained, "I make the garlic aioli myself. It's a special recipe. Actually, it was given to me by one of my former patients, Bernice. Very sweet lady."

It made Keldon sad, *sweet*-sad to think of Josh's former client, obviously deceased, and her delicious garlic aioli still being celebrated and appreciated near the Thai pavilion in a botanical garden. *Your aioli lives on, Bernice*, he thought to himself.

Josh said, "Hey, do we have to talk about the painting situation at all today? Is that a thing we have to do?"

Keldon paused and looked around, the fresh green grass, the the smell of turned flower beds, a promise of beauty yet to come. "I probably should, but I'd rather not. I mean, we don't have to."

"Good," Josh said. "That's good. Let's just have a date."

"I like you," Keldon said.

He was surprised by the simplicity of those words and equally surprised to hear them burst so casually from his mouth. Everything in his dating history told him to play it more cautious, see how interested his partner was first before sharing at that level. But there they were, the words already spoken.

"We'll see about that," Josh said, "after I share this afternoon's plans. Manual labor."

"Manual labor, huh?"

"I'm not kidding. I have work for us to do in my backyard." Josh paused. "And I like you too."

They ate their sandwiches slowly, and Keldon expressed his disappointment that the bread wasn't incredibly dry and flaky, like breakfast. Josh laughed. Already, a small pile of inside jokes accumulated between them. But all too soon, the pear slices disappeared, and the Doritos were devoured. They folded the tablecloth, repacking it with the remaining couscous in Josh's bicycle bags. While wandering under the intricately carved pavilion once more before leaving, Josh produced a box with four chocolate squares, a sampler from a local confectionary, a business he was sure practiced the dark magic arts to make them taste so good. Keldon savored a silky dark chocolate with an orange-tasting interior and then stopped chewing to close his eyes and let the experience melt all over his tongue. He'd tasted chocolate this sophisticated in France, but that was the last time he remembered being moved to silence.

Without words, he offered the other half to Josh, who said, "No, go ahead. Finish it."

Keldon leaned in to kiss Josh, and they did, tasting the remnants of each other's chocolate. The kiss lengthened into something else, a passionate embrace, and they held each other under the Thai pavilion.

When they broke apart, Josh said, "Wow. The chocolate was that good, huh?"

Keldon finally found words and said, "Yeah. That good."

* * * *

After biking back to Josh's home and dispatching the remains of their lunch, Josh outlined the afternoon's activity: assembling a new raised flower bed to contain tomatoes. Keldon counted four raised beds already in existence, but Josh explained that, to a veteran gardener, four was hardly sufficient.

"This isn't my main vegetable garden. This is just my laboratory. I keep trying to find sturdier broccoli that doesn't wither the minute it's too hot. Once I grew cantaloupe here. The melons I got were tasty but not worth how much space they occupied."

Keldon held a shovel in his hand and wondered what the hell he would be expected to do. "You really weren't kidding about the manual labor."

"I'm sure glad you agreed to two dates," Josh said, grinning.

For the remainder of the afternoon, they dug. They dragged. Josh shared his calculations, his vision, what he hoped to see when they finished. Keldon dug where he was asked to dig, moved dirt, and twice even made suggestions for the bed construction, more about aesthetics than practical value, but he found himself involved. Caring, perhaps. Josh was enthusiastic the entire time, laughing, goofing, teasing Keldon that he wished it were warmer so they'd have a good reason to take off their shirts. They spent the last hour planting six tomato plants and three cherry tomato plants, all outlined in a crisp marigold border, which Josh explained would stink up the bed enough to keep lusting critters away. For a while, at least. The marigolds shared the same colors as the morning's tulips, a sharp yellow streaked with oranges bordering on red. But their crinkled, grimacing faces could not match the tranquility of the tulips, the two dozen bobbing in the early morning breeze as Keldon remembered them, their smooth planes nodding with deference.

When they finished in the late afternoon, Keldon felt an odd satisfaction, realizing that even if he and Josh never saw each other again, he would have impacted Josh's life by participating in this project. It wasn't significant, he knew that, but he was part of this yard now, this average yard on an average block in the middle of America. He had planted a little piece of himself.

They stood and admired the afternoon's work.

"Looks good," Keldon said.

"Thanks for the idea to plant the raised side out," Josh said.

"I just thought it would look better from the house."

"Thank you," Josh said.

Keldon noticed Josh's voice was husky but didn't know how to read the underlying emotion.

Josh turned and walked toward the house. "You take a shower first, and I'll start getting some dinner stuff going. I want to roll out the scones and throw together the salad. Clean towels are in the hall linen closet."

He watched Josh walk back to the house, puzzled by the almost-sadness in Josh's voice. Keldon entered the house, and Josh worked with his back to him, ignoring his presence. Confused and mildly alarmed, Keldon entered the bathroom. The shower was exactly what he wanted, hot water firing over his skin, almost burning the soreness off his muscles. After the physical relief soaked through his body, his mind traveled elsewhere, wondering if he had done something wrong, misread a joke or misspoke. There was no point in pretending something had not changed. Keldon knew how to read the signs. But he didn't know what it meant, how he had screwed up.

He dressed, spent a little extra time in front of the mirror making sure he looked good in his faded jeans and his printed T-shirt endorsing a laundry soap from forty years ago. He decided to wear comfortable clothes, the ones he would never wear on a date. He hoped Josh would like his appearance, his outfit, though he scolded himself not to care.

In the kitchen, still wet behind the --ears, Keldon found an open bottle of wine on the egg-white-colored tile counter, and under a wine glass, a note suggesting, "Help yourself." He poured himself a glass. He caught sight of Josh in the backyard, standing near the raised bed, his wineglass bulb resting in the palm of his hand.

Keldon raised the glass, smelled it as Steven had taught him, and was not terribly impressed. He knew good wine from mediocre, and this was definitely mediocre. But he took a sip and decided he didn't mind it as much as he thought. Without putting on shoes or socks, he walked out the back door and joined Josh.

"Hey," Keldon said.

The two men stood in silence watching tomato plants.

Josh cleared his throat. "I'm sorry I got weird a minute ago. I kinda just walked away from you right after we finished." He paused and sipped his wine. "Here's the thing. I don't date much. I used to when I was more normal, more like Mr. Nine-to-Five. Go out for a movie, for coffee, go look in shop windows. But then I got too eccentric for most guys. Sure, the farmers' market is fun once or twice in the summer to get some freshly baked bread or nice green beans. It's cute. But I go every week to get the food that's going to feed me. The farmers' market is not a chore— it's something I love. I go early every week because it's important to me, more than sleeping in on a Saturday. If you're not into it the way I am, this way of eating and living, the farmers' market isn't much fun the third week in a row."

Keldon nodded but wasn't sure where this was headed.

Josh sipped his wine.

"When you proposed we go on a date," Josh said, "the first thing I realized, well, two things, was that first, maybe you had a spark of interest in me after all. That thrilled me. And that made me bold enough for the second realization I had, almost instantly, that I could make you, this hot guy, go on a date doing stuff *I* liked. Farmers' market. Making a home-cooked meal. Biking somewhere beautiful for a lunch and even working together doing manual labor. So I insisted we have a second date."

Keldon smiled.

Josh looked at Keldon with earnestness in his eyes. "I'm really grateful to you for today. I've never had a date like this. Even if you hated every minute of it, you *acted* like you enjoyed it, which meant one of two things. The first is you're a really good actor when it comes to dating. Or the second possibility is that maybe you actually enjoyed today and this stands out as one of the really fun dates in my life. So if you hated today and were just acting, don't say anything. Keep acting. Because I'm having fun today. This is better than what I had hoped for."

Keldon felt humbled by this admission and felt like saying, "Me too," but it seemed too easy and trite. He wanted to communicate that the date was *different* for him, too, something unusual and happily unexpected.

Keldon said, "I am a good actor on dates. I know how to react the right way to what a guy wants. That's one of the reasons I didn't want to talk about my dating past. I didn't always like who I was then. It's easy for me to pretend I love whatever the other guy wants. But I'm not acting today. That's what makes this date different for me. I'm not acting. I've had a *great* day with you."

Josh held out his glass with a nervous smile.

Keldon clinked it, and they toasted without words. It felt too soon to express much more emotion than what now lay exposed, so he did what good men do when they don't want to talk further. He pointed at what they had built together, discussing its minor successes and even smaller flaws, avoiding saying anything too emotional.

The sun, while still visible above the horizon, had clearly begun its descent. The soft twilight crickets began warming up their instruments. The two men finished their first glass of wine and returned into the house for more. While in the kitchen, Josh produced speakers to connect to his smartphone and picked a playlist for their evening dinner music.

Keldon teased him. "I thought your phone was only for work and emergencies."

"Pot roast *is* an emergency."

While Motown classics permeated the kitchen, the fragrant roast aroma also fought for air space, so the music and meat compromised and danced around the enclosed space together, getting both men drunk on sensations. The potatoes were soon mashed and the scones arranged on a cookie sheet, ready to be plunked into the oven. Together, they tossed the salad, poured more wine, cut up an orange, and licked each other's fingers while doing so, stopping to kiss or rub each other's head every minute or two, the way lovers do after they have admitted the spark is real.

The first five minutes of dinner was spent chewing and moaning quietly, nodding at each other and pointing at the food with forks. The rest of the meal, they discussed the pot roast, the spices, the way meat and its juices create succulent bases for a number of different sauces and cooking experiments. Their mutual love for good foods bound them closer together. Josh thanked him again for his hours of service in the yard, raising a toast, but this time with happy gratitude, not overly emotional but fraught with good cheer.

"Here's the thing about manual labor." Josh smacked his lips and cut another small slice of roast. "Here, have a little more. Anyway, I was going to say that you can spend four hours chatting in a coffee shop and it still won't tell you much about your date. Work with someone for an hour, digging, planting, building a chicken coop. Whatever. Work a task with unclear parameters other than to get it done and you'll figure out the man at your side."

"Oh yeah?"

"Yup," Josh said, chewing. "You didn't complain. You didn't bitch. You didn't say, 'how much longer do we have to do this?' which is what one guy said to me. We had dated for a month, and I asked him to help me garden one Saturday. Pull weeds. I asked him to *help* me. Which was a big mistake, turns out."

Keldon said, "I thought if I complained, you wouldn't let me have pot roast. And even by, like, three this afternoon, it was starting to smell really damn good."

Josh laughed. "I know, right?"

After dinner, Josh dropped the scones into the oven and set his smartphone's timer for twelve minutes.

"Put on your shoes," Josh said. "We have twelve minutes for a short walk around the block. Let's go."

They hurried while inside, but once out in the May twilight, they slowed down and began a comfortable pace down the sidewalk.

"I can't believe how light it is right now. I can still see sunlight."

"I think the sun officially set a few minutes ago," Josh said.

"It's nice," Keldon said and yawned. "Although, wow, this is a long day. Action-packed."

"Which is why I go to bed so early," Josh said. "It's amazing I'm not more ripped and buff given how much I do outside."

"You're buff enough," Keldon said. "I've seen you with your shirt off. Buff enough."

Josh chuckled. "Thank you. I probably should confess that I have other guilty pleasures besides KFC. I like Arby's potato triangles."

"Ugh," Keldon said. "I knew it. I knew you were a big fake."

They teased each other gently until Josh checked the phone's timer and suggested they turn around and head back.

He said, "Making it around the full block in twelve minutes was probably a little too ambitious."

Keldon asked, "How did you end up as a nurse in Madison? Sounded like you were living in New York City and working there."

"Yeah," Josh said. "I was. I grew up in a couple different places but moved to New York for art school. After that, I became a graphic artist at a big pharmaceutical company. They paid really well. I mean, I wasn't rich in New York, but I only had one job, which is saying something. But I didn't like it. The work was tedious and constrained by a billion branding requirements, so

I rarely created something original. I would get high praise for refitting their logo to a new size or something ridiculous. The best part of my day was walking to work from the subway because I spent that time outside. Short version, I asked for the transfer to Madison because I wanted to begin school as a nurse. The company would reimburse me as long as I got a degree related to the pharmaceutical industry. They were kind of reluctant to transition me at first because I was an asset as a graphic designer. But I convinced them I could be even more valuable if I understood nursing. I dunno why, but they went for it."

"You didn't like being a graphic artist?"

"Sometimes it was fun," Josh said. "But graphics lie. They'd want me to invent a way to visually display disappointing numbers, delivering bad news in a 'less negative light.' What they *really* wanted was a misleading graphic disguising how bad the projections were. They would never say it directly, but that's what they wanted, and if I didn't do it, they'd keep saying shit like, 'No, that's not quite right.' I hated it. I hated them trying to make it my responsibility to tell their lies. With greater frequency, I kept being asked to create these internal-use-only images, these bullshit lies, and the worst part was they always wanted me to help brainstorm the best way to mislead. The corporate world will suck out your soul."

"And you quit when you finished nursing school."

"I quit my last semester of school. I couldn't take the work bullshit, most of college was paid for, and I needed to get serious about my finals and internships, stuff like that. I used my savings to pay my bills while I finished my degree. And five years later, here I am."

"Here you are. Since you like farming so much, why didn't you do something more outside, like become a landscape architect?" Keldon asked.

"I thought about it. I didn't feel like art school turned out well. I ended up working for people I didn't like, on products I didn't believe in, and I didn't want to make another hobby I loved into a career. Plus, I love nursing. I like working with sick people."

Keldon was surprised. He didn't often hear people talk about loving what they do with enthusiasm. Both Steven and Aamir discussed work as a necessary evil to accomplish the true goal: get money.

"It's a cool story. And you didn't miss New York?"

"I did. I do, some things. But not much. I love this. I love we just spent ten minutes on this gorgeous evening strolling around the block. And without trash or smells or even seeing another person except that woman walking her dog, the—"

"Yeah," Keldon said. "I saw her. With the hair."

"Yes," Josh said enthusiastically. "Did you see how big that hair was? Wow. That was something else. Anyway, I love this. We're going to my place and having scones drizzled with blueberry crème. From blueberries I picked last summer. This is what I love. I was never a New Yorker. I think I've always been a Madison guy before I even knew about this place."

They reached Josh's front porch, and Keldon stopped him from going in. "How much time did that take?"

Josh pulled out his phone. "We have about a minute before the timer goes off. Why?"

Keldon said, "Perfect."

He pulled Josh close. They circled their arms around each other, and standing in front of Josh's home, they kissed in the last minute of sunlight.

* * * *

While happily munching the golden-brown scones with their cool, sugary drizzle, Keldon made a decision. He would tell Josh about the James Wayne Merrick painting. He would reveal his true mission. Whether tonight or tomorrow morning, time would tell. But it felt right. Keldon felt safe here. Irene refused to sell without understanding the situation. Mrs. Maggiarra wanted that painting. Relief flooded through him as he realized it was time to tell. That meant throughout their shared Saturday, when he never tried to manipulate or 'work' Josh, unconsciously, his mind was working through this decision. That pleased him, thinking that he had an unconscious wisdom that trumped his attempts to please his partner. Perhaps there was hope for him yet.

He had begun to think through the ramifications of a third, fourth, and possibly fifth date with Josh, the challenges they would face as Keldon tried to discover how much of 'the pioneer lifestyle' he could tolerate. Added into the equation were his own subtractions, meaning Keldon could not afford to date. He could not afford rental cars and tanks of gas to Madison and buying dinners out. The weekly stipend Mrs. Maggiarra paid him was generous enough to cover living expenses and dent his forest of credit card debt. Paying the rent two months in advance helped smooth things over with an angry landlord. But there wasn't much surplus.

He tried not to dwell on future dates, or he'd miss out on the second date, the one right now, the date where they each ate a second scone while in the backyard, revisiting their afternoon's construction. It was almost nighttime dark.

"Firefly," Josh said, pointing.

"Firefly!" Keldon said, echoing with delight.

He would tell Josh in the morning. He didn't want to ruin tonight.

Drunk with exhaustion brought on by physical exertion, great food, and intense feeling, the two men stumbled to Josh's bedroom and stripped, murmuring sexy admiration for each other's underwear-clad bodies. They exchanged a few drowsy kisses that led nowhere and lay content in each other's arms until their half-sentence mumblings were doused by sleep.

Chapter Seven

Keldon woke to a scent not his own, one coming from the pillow. Josh was gone. The thought made him realize he wasn't in his own bed, and he stretched out, allowing his eyes to explore while he felt the pleasant soreness from yesterday's exertions. He heard something from another room, a kitchen noise, which meant Josh wasn't far. The bedroom was plain, like Josh's other rooms, but Keldon tried harder to appreciate the economy of furniture, the practicality of everything on display. Atop the dresser Keldon could see spare change and a few scraps of paper, receipts perhaps. The lacy white curtains did little to break the sunlight, which suggested to Keldon's awakening brain that perhaps he was rising earlier than he wanted. Perhaps he should go back to sleep.

But it was no use. He was awake and almost naked in a hot guy's bed. He would not return to sleep. Something had been about to happen last night, the promise of exploratory sex, which Keldon realized he most desperately wanted. He was damn ready. But nope, they'd slept.

It didn't bother Keldon because he could still smell Joshua's scent, he basked in it, the warm sheets, the streaming morning light, remembering a day well spent. He remembered his favorite part, the walk around the block, the light fading, the normalcy of a short stroll timed to coincide with dessert in the oven. Or maybe he only loved that moment because it represented the closure of a great day, a fantastic day. And he hadn't had one of those in a while. Who knew he could find that kind of pleasure while putting together a vegetable bed? He decided to throw away the assumption suggesting manual labor was a chore.

Keldon mused and heard soft music, morning music piped in through the iPod, loud at first, then adjusted to much quieter almost instantly, as if Josh were protecting his last minutes of sleep.

"Heeeeeeeeeeeeeeeeeeeey," Keldon said in a loud groan that doubled as stretching.

Josh appeared in the doorway, shirtless, wearing a blue denim apron.

"Hey yourself. How'd you sleep?"

"Like a rock. I'm having a hard time waking up. What time is it?"

"You don't want to know."

"Early? Is it before eight?"

"Earlier. If you want, you could go back to sleep."

Keldon rose on his elbow. "I'm up."

Josh unsnapped the apron strap from around his neck and then released the drawstrings tied behind his back. "I'll take that as an invitation."

"It was," Keldon said, "although I'd like to brush my teeth first."

Josh threw the apron to the wood floor and said, "You know what will help you get that taste out of your mouth?" He stripped off his underwear next and kicked it across the room. "Sucking dick."

Keldon was surprised to see how quickly Josh was naked and equally glad he had reason to shuck his own shorts. He was also surprised Josh was so forthright, so suddenly dirty and demanding. He liked it. Aamir had approached sex with a certain aggression, and Keldon had liked that too.

Traditionally, sex had always been fraught with right and wrong choices for Keldon, nipples that shouldn't be touched or tweaked but at the right moments, twisted hard. Discovering the difference between too much suction and not enough was a narrow road to navigate. Steven was very particular about what Keldon did with his hands during sex. Aamir's cock was very sensitive.

The idea of sex with Josh left Keldon eager, but nervous too. He didn't want to do sex wrong or in a way that displeased Josh, but he also was conscious of giving himself permission to do it differently to focus on his own pleasure, not just his partner's.

Josh approached the bed, his hard dick leading the way. He grinned at Keldon. "I'm assuming you want this. Do you?"

Keldon smirked without answering and scooted closer to the edge of the bed. A flash of panic raced through him for the unknowns in having sex with someone new. The panic fled when he cupped Josh's balls, covered in blond-brown hairs, feeling their warmth, and hearing Josh moan. That moan reminded him he did know what he was doing; sexually, he could bring pleasure. Everything would be okay.

He inhaled the scent, the fresh rawness of cock, and, without giving it further thought, took the head inside his mouth. Josh groaned louder, the good kind of groaning, and Keldon allowed instinct to take over. He explored Josh through his dick, discovering things about the man, like how much attention he craved, how much pressure he liked. Josh had explained last night about the value of manual labor to discover another man's true qualities. Keldon could make the same argument for sex. Was he demanding in bed? Could he surrender to new sensations? Did he have to direct the show, or could he roll with a new technique and a new mouth's skills? Josh seemed to be the let-go-and-enjoy type, folding his arms behind his skull and lifting his chin to the ceiling, allowing Keldon free access to suck, slurp, and massage his balls. Keldon used his free hand to gently rub Josh's stomach.

They continued this way until Josh pulled away slightly, which disappointed Keldon. He hadn't sucked dick in a very long time and was just beginning to find his groove.

"Getting too close," Josh hissed and stepped back. "You're incredible. This is incredible. I have to stop for a moment. It's been so long since I had sex, and you're really turning me on."

Keldon wiped his lower lip and smirked. "We don't *have* to stop…"

Josh laughed and pounced, straddling him and rubbing his hard, spit-covered dick against Keldon's.

"If we kept going," Josh said, "I couldn't do this, could I?"

He continued to rub himself against Keldon. The sensations were confusing and perfect. He felt the heft of Josh's body without the weight of it. He felt the wetness of Josh's cock when it pressed against his own and smelled the slight masculine scent from his armpits, a heavenly aroma. Balanced on his elbows, Josh smiled down at him, a sexy, wicked grin that suggested this frottage could head in any number of possible directions next. Keldon couldn't anticipate Josh's next move as much as he'd like, as much as he wanted, so he surrendered to the moment the best he could, feeling the warmth of a new lover.

Josh kissed him, still grinding on top of him, squirming against him, and the sensations on his mouth, his dick, the hands caressing his sides overwhelmed him. The kiss was passionate, wet, grateful, hungry. Keldon held on, grabbing Josh's meaty ass cheeks. They rolled, and Keldon found himself on top, sword-fighting, wet sword-fighting, kissing with curiosity, exploring each other's taste, and discovering what elicited the biggest reactions from each other. Keldon chewed gently on Josh's lower lip, and Josh sighed with the kind of satisfaction that communicates, *You found one of my magic spots.*

There were fumbles, Keldon's knee accidentally digging into Josh's side, and Josh's armpit kiss elicited more of a laughter burst than a pleasurable sensation, which made both of them giggle, appreciating the newness of sex with someone unfamiliar. But the awkwardness was welcome too, the missteps and kisses that simply didn't end at the same time. Each confused hand placement and accidental kiss meant a desire to explore further, to understand.

Each misstep was forgiven since each originated from the desire to bring surprising pleasure.

Keldon discovered Josh liked sucking the tip of his tongue, and Keldon discovered he liked that too.

Josh kissed his way down Keldon's hairless chest, down his stomach, and he allowed his jaw to graze Keldon's dark pubes. Keldon's mouth opened wide, but no sound came out as Josh took him, all of him, into his mouth in one swoop. Keldon didn't make much noise during sex, didn't know if he could, really. Steven hadn't liked overt groaning and moaning, and since he was Keldon's first, Keldon had suppressed any natural instincts to make noise, if they existed. He didn't know if he *wanted* to make noise.

But he knew he liked this. Josh's wet attention, sucking in long slurps from tip to base made his head thrash and his fingers search out Josh's broad shoulders. He loved his hands on Josh, grabbing the neck muscles and holding them, which elicited a stronger groan from Josh. Keldon's mouth formed the letter O, though no noise emerged, but he jerked his head from left to right and folded his legs over the middle of Josh's back. When Josh sucked to the base and kept his mouth there, Keldon whimpered and then cried out. He obviously had the potential to make some noise.

Josh continued until Keldon thrashed harder against the warm sheets, and a low, guttural moan emerged, signaling his readiness to shoot.

"Josh," he said, gasping. "Oh god…"

He meant to say more, but could not. He came, and Josh held on, taking the pulsing cock into his throat, sucking it, the unbelievable warmth and power of the moment enough to make Keldon buck his hips harder, push straight into Josh, who seemed determined to never let go. But Josh did free himself mere seconds later, and Keldon understood why when he saw Josh rear up, and saw the blur of Josh's fist jacking his own cock as he had probably been doing while sucking Keldon. Josh groaned and creamed Keldon's midsection, his pubes, and eventually dribbled the last two spurts right on Keldon's softening dick.

Josh slow-motion crashed on top of Keldon, letting his arms hit the bed, and then rolled off to the side, so both men lay on their backs and panted.

They turned their heads and grinned at each other, eyeing the spent cocks, spittle, and sweat pools on each other, not bothering to speak, Keldon proud of how they navigated the potentially awkward sexual experience. This level of enthusiasm and connectedness was definitely a good sign. Josh grinned at the ceiling, and Keldon felt joy.

"Better get us a towel," Keldon suggested.

"In a minute." Josh leered, and they pressed their bodies together to feel the slippery mess between them, enjoying long kisses in the shadow of their first lovemaking.

They entered the bathroom together.

Though Keldon had hoped they would shower together, Josh hopped behind the curtain and said, "Sorry about going first. It's rude since you're my guest, but while you're showering, I'll start cooking our blueberry pancakes. Everything's mixed up and ready to go."

The rationale pleased Keldon. No one had made him breakfast before. Not Steven. Not Aamir. Keldon knew he and Josh would have other chances to shower together. While he felt confident of that before falling asleep the previous night, he felt it even stronger this morning in the sticky.

True to his words, Josh didn't take long, just a quick rinsing. He grabbed Keldon before Keldon could step under the spray. He kissed him deeply, and Keldon inhaled the fresh clean scent of a man, a scent that woke his slumbering cock for a second round. It had been a while since Keldon enjoyed sex.

"I need food before round two," Josh said, smiling and cupping Keldon's balls.

Keldon quivered, and his dick grew harder.

"I like where this is going." Josh stroked Keldon's balls gently. "So hold that thought."

He dashed out of the bathroom, and Keldon called after him, "Cock tease!"

Keldon compared his shower at Josh's to the day prior at the Madison Concourse hotel. The hotel showerhead was a rainforest showerhead. The water was hotter, the shower more spacious, allowing steam to billow and envelop him. But today's post-sex shower felt better, felt more amazing. The water planed over his sore muscles, washing away the scent of sex. Unbidden, the phrase *dirty whore* raced through his mind, but this time he chuckled at it and thought, *Not today. Not today.*

Keldon threw on yesterday's T-shirt with his underwear and joined Josh in the kitchen. While dressing he'd realized he could now tell Josh about the painting. Josh could either relate the news to Irene himself or invite Keldon to explain the true origins of her sister's art.

The scent of a fresh, warm breakfast made Keldon feel buoyant and light.

While Josh poured them orange juice, Keldon cleared his throat and announced he needed to explain something. It wouldn't take long. As he said that phrase, a twang thumped his heart, a sudden fear that perhaps—*maybe*—this wouldn't go well. He hadn't fully explored that possibility. He assumed the freedom of knowing the painting's origin would be a relief to both Irene and Josh.

He said, "I got Mrs. Maggiarra's permission to tell you and Irene which painting."

Josh grinned. "Oh really? Cool. But first, let me share something."

Keldon nodded. He watched Josh pour two more pancakes into the heavy black skillet and then noticed the four already on a plate, thick and boasting purple berries.

Once the pancakes were cooking and bubbling, Josh said, "We've been trying so damn hard to figure out which painting you guys want. Irene's convinced one of the paintings has another painting behind it, like an original that's been painted over. That's her theory. We spent time trying to track down the origins of a few, but none of them are honestly that exclusive. The upstairs swans painting cost them a few grand but nothing outrageous She and I have had a lot of fun doing research together."

Keldon smiled weakly. "No, no. No one famous. Well, maybe. Kind of famous. But not in a good way."

Keldon explained his employer, Mrs. Maggiarra and her unusual desire to collect James Wayne Merrick's art. Josh had been tending the blueberry pancakes, lifting the edges to see if they were ready to flip, but he stopped as Keldon explained his position as art curator. There wasn't much to tell, Keldon discovered. Josh watched him with mild astonishment.

"I can't explain Mrs. Maggiarra's actions very well," Keldon said. "Why she tried to keep it a secret from Irene. Almost everyone I've dealt with wanted more money than Mrs. Maggiarra has originally offered them, but by the time it's done, they take the original price or even less. Mrs. Maggiarra's offer to Irene was a lot more than anyone else got offered, and I mean *a lot* more. She wasn't trying to cheat Irene. Nobody got offered that kind of money, and you're my fifth acquisition."

Josh nodded, seeming to take this in. "I was your fifth acquisition."

Something about the edge in those words set off Keldon's alarms. He suddenly realized Josh might not handle this news well.

"No, not you. The painting. The Merrick painting Irene believes her sister painted."

"And Irene's sister didn't paint it. You guys are sure?"

"Yes," Keldon said, suddenly realizing the seriousness of this situation. "Mrs. Maggiarra has investigators—"

"Quit calling her that," Josh said, and his face grew darker. "We call my friend 'Irene', but your friend 'Mrs. Maggiarra,' like she's some big shot, when in fact she's this sicko collecting serial-killer art."

Keldon hesitated. "She's not my friend. She's my employer."

"This is your *job*," Josh said, almost in anguish. "You collect *serial-killer art*."

Hearing it come from Josh's mouth like that frightened Keldon. He thought the connection shared on their Madison date would protect him, would protect *them* from any fallout. He was wrong. This was about to go very badly. He knew that now. The best he could do at this moment was answer questions in a straightforward way.

Josh took a few steps in one direction and turned. "Do you know what she's going to do with them?"

"Catherine hasn't said." Keldon hoped calling her by her first name would earn him something, an extra moment longer in conversation, the opportunity to explain how desperately he needed the money.

"Oh my god." Josh stepped away from the oven, putting his hands to his face.

Keldon watched him, nauseated, recognizing how he had underestimated this situation, the impact of this reveal.

"This is worse than I could have imagined," Josh said. "I mean, this is amazing. You don't even know what she's going to do with these paintings. She might be building a museum or putting together a gallery show so that this guy's art is seen all over the world. Did you think of that?"

"I've thought about a lot of things," Keldon said cautiously, finding a spark of his own frustration, "including how I couldn't afford the next month's rent before I met Catherine. I don't have options. To be honest, I ate better food with you yesterday than I do most days of the year. Trust me, I don't love this job. But I am broke and desperate."

"I know," Josh said, and his unhappiness was palpable in the room. "Yeah, I get it. Tough choices. But Jesus, there's a line. And collecting serial-killer art is way over that line, especially when you don't even know why the fuck you're doing it. Or for whom."

"I'm not supposed to ask." As soon as he said the words, he realized how weak they sounded. "One of the conditions of my contract is that I can't—"

"Stop," Josh said, backing away. "I don't want to hear any more. This is too much. It's too much. I can't see you again."

They stood in shocked silence at the words as they hung between them.

"Josh," Keldon said, pleading. "We—"

"Your job is to collect serial-killer art," Josh said, and his eyes grew wider as if he just fully understood the words himself. "No. Just, no."

Keldon involuntarily glanced at the blueberry pancakes in the skillet. They would never get flipped, it seemed. They would never reach fruition, not this morning. The blueberry pancakes on the plate grew colder.

"I'm gonna get dressed," Josh said, "and leave. I'm not going to Irene's house because I don't know how I'm going to tell her this or how she'll react. I'm going to bike somewhere and think. But here's what I want. I want you to be gone by the time I get back. Eat some pancakes if you want, but I'm serious. Please be gone. This is way too fucked-up."

"Wait," Keldon said. "At least let me—"

"No." Josh backed away. "I can't do this. *Serial-killer art*, Keldon. How the hell did you think I would react?"

Keldon's face grew red. "I'm not the serial killer. And I'm not forming a collection of this stuff. I'm not even the investigator on this. I go and present a check and pick up a painting, and I help talk people through their doubts about selling it or holding out for more money. I'm not thrilled about this work either, you know. But I don't want to be homeless."

Josh put his hands to his eyes.

"I never finished college," Keldon said. "I don't have any work skills."

Josh turned away and headed into the bedroom. In less than three minutes, the front door slammed shut.

Through the back window, Keldon stared at the raised garden bed they'd created together and returned to the bedroom to gather his things.

Chapter Eight

Keldon called Catherine Maggiarra from the rental car. He didn't want to. He wanted to wait until he planned his next step but considered that Irene could conceivably call Catherine any minute with rage or with questions. Although Josh said he was not headed to Irene's house, Keldon couldn't risk the chance Josh changed his mind. He couldn't let Catherine get ambushed. He explained an abridged version of how Keldon had revealed the truth about Merrick's painting. They discussed the next move toward acquisition. It was Catherine who counseled patience.

"Give it a week," she said. "And then I'll call Irene myself. See if there's anything to be done. You're sure you don't know how she responded?"

Keldon did not. "Josh said he wasn't going to her house to tell her right away. Maybe he was. I don't know. He was furious when he left."

"Let me know if you hear anything," Catherine said. "If he calls you and you have any insight to what she's thinking or how she's leaning, let me know."

"I will," Keldon promised. "I'll call Josh in a few hours to see if he'll talk to me."

"Be careful," Catherine said. "Don't overcall and spook him. This is a delicate time in negotiations."

Keldon contemplated how she could have no idea how personal this had become. She possessed no concept of how amazing the two dates had been and how much Keldon ached for the warm blueberry pancakes, the ones they ate together, followed by making love again. It wasn't just the morning itself he wanted back, but the feeling, the closeness. It was the first genuine connection he had made in a year. He wanted to call Josh forty times that day.

After another moment of silence, Catherine abruptly began explaining Acquisition Number Seven, another of Merrick's prison pen pals.

Keldon found himself feeling quarrelsome with Catherine even though she had not contributed to the mess he'd created. "Mrs. Maggiarra. Catherine. I need a day or two off. I'm sorry. This took a toll on me, and I'd like to just have the next two days off. I need a break."

"Of course." She got quiet. "Are you all right?"

"I'm fine," he said and wanted to explain he was not. But she was not his friend. She was his employer. "It was kinda rough. I was invested in this, and now I don't know how to fix it."

"It'll fix itself," she said.

Keldon said nothing.

"You'll see," Catherine said. "Mrs. Woullet may be as upset as Joshua, but she'll come around. And who knows? She may not be upset at all. The money is more than fair, and she has bills. She can be morally outraged, but she'll sell. We might just have to give this one a little time. She has a daughter. I might have you meet with her, see if she's persuadable."

The idea made Keldon sick to his stomach, but he said, "You're probably right. We'll just wait a few days and see what happens."

They ended the call with that false optimism, and Keldon found himself hating her a little more. How could he have so grossly underestimated Josh's reaction? How could he have not known? Didn't it make Keldon sick to his stomach to wheedle, flatter, and negotiate for the art? Had he become so blasé about his loathsome job that he forgot most people would also find any connection to serial killers abnormal and abhorrent?

Keldon wanted another date. He wanted Josh. He wanted to see Josh's sexy grin and smell the pancakes again.

Maybe Josh would return his calls.

* * * *

Phone messages were not returned. By the time he pressed the digits for his fourth call in two days, Keldon felt there was nothing sadder than calling a man you felt something for, knowing he did not wish to hear from you. Keldon hadn't dated anyone in a year and a half, but he had never felt lonelier than he did dialing Josh, knowing he would not pick up.

Still, he couldn't stop himself from dialing.

Keldon passed the time talking himself out of wanting to hear from Josh again. He reminded himself he had no business beginning a relationship, the one he could not afford to maintain. He did not know if he could live with Josh's lifestyle, the one where he got to see Josh's excitement over flower beds and stronger tomato breeds. The relationship where they fell asleep together, exhausted. It had been a good exhausted, even if it were only a day. All Keldon's arguments for not engaging in a relationship ended with him staring into Josh's eyes over lemon scones with fresh blueberry crème.

He tortured himself looking for apartments in Madison and was shocked to discover just how much cheaper the rent was than Chicago. If only he had a good enough reason to move.

* * * *

Five days had passed when his phone rang. Keldon felt the vibration in his pocket and worried he had missed Josh, but at that moment he was deeply engaged in conversation with another acquisition, a second meeting with Acquisition Number Seven, hoping to make better headway than the first interaction. The owners promised they had another interested party, though

Keldon was sure it was a bluff. Nevertheless, they wanted a higher bid. His ruse texting Mrs. Maggiarra disguised as Mr. Mercer did not meet with immediate success.

Once out of the house, he walked toward the Metra station, the one that would take him from the suburbs back to his Chicago apartment, and once he was confident he was no longer in view of the home he had just visited, he pulled out his cell phone and frowned at the unfamiliar number. When he heard the voicemail begin, "This is Irene Woullet," he almost threw up. He listened to her message three times to make sure he heard the words correctly. She invited him to show up at her house the next day to collect the desired painting. She explained that he did not need to bring her a cashier's check as she would be donating the painting free of charge. The message was curt.

He decided not to tell Catherine Maggiarra, not until he could hand her the painting itself and see her face. He wanted to see her reaction. Of course, he would have to acquire the painting, and something suggested it would not be as easy as Irene had promised. Maybe it would. Maybe she didn't want to possess the serial-killer art any more than Josh wanted to be in the same room with him. Maybe disgust was the strongest emotion, transcending greed or the need for money. Despite his weak relief for a solution to Acquisition Number Five, Keldon almost didn't care. With Irene's situation resolved, he had no more reason to visit Madison. He might never see Josh again. He was sad Josh didn't call himself to relay the news.

* * * *

He rented a car and drove to Madison with an upset stomach, dreading each mile. He pulled over after crossing the Wisconsin state line, headed to the first rest stop, though he felt no urge to rest or stop. He just needed a break, to walk around the car and gain some confidence. He was sure Josh would be present, sitting at Irene's side. He was sure of it.

Best-case scenario, Keldon decided, was the painting sitting in a plastic bag on the front stoop. Also, that was the worst-case scenario, where Keldon never got to see Josh again.

When Keldon arrived at the Woullet address, he dreaded the sight of the gorgeous home so close to the lake. The rich chocolate exterior surrounded by pines and other trees' effusive green leaves could not lift his spirits. He scanned the porch and did not see anything that looked like a package for him, making him both relieved and experience greater dread.

Though he was five minutes early, Keldon could not wait a second longer. He walked to the house, reminding himself to breathe.

Before he could knock or ring the bell, Josh opened the door and looked at him unhappily. "Come in."

Keldon remembered their first meeting less than a month ago, almost a month ago, actually, so oddly similar in unhappy greeting. Josh turned as if he expected Keldon to follow. He did, of course, but choked back an innate desire to kiss Josh, to throw his arms around him and say, "I'm sorry."

They walked in unnatural silence to the library. There was no tea service for him this time. He could not tell if the books were stacked exactly the same way, overflowing shelves and on tables and stacks on the floor, but he was fairly certain nothing had moved since the last visit.

"Hello, Keldon," Irene said, no edge to her voice, no barb, but no friendliness either.

Keldon nodded and asked if he should sit.

"Yes, please." She indicated a chair with her head. "My hands aren't working well today. Otherwise I would have not have asked Joshua to be here. I did ask him because I can't hand you the bag myself."

Josh sat in the chair next to her and looked at Keldon with a forlorn expression. A kicked dog.

"Just to recap my understanding," Irene said. "Mrs. Maggiarra buys serial-killer art from whoever owns it."

"Yes. James Wayne Merrick's art."

"And is it multiple serial killers or just this one?"

"Just this one. I think. I guess. I honestly don't know, ma'am."

"And you don't know why Mrs. Maggiarra hasn't explained to you what you're doing."

"That's correct." Keldon had been looking her in the eye, letting her see his honesty and his sorrow over this experience, but he could not take her unflinching stare any longer. He looked away. "I am contractually forbidden from asking questions about her intentions. I think she wants it that way so that I can't accidentally reveal something while on one of her assignments. People want to know what her plans are. I can answer everyone honestly, because I do not know. She probably won't ever tell me. And she prefers I am the contact for each acquisition so they won't have access to her directly. She was willing to speak with you because you were the exception to the rule. You didn't know you possessed a Merrick painting."

"Yes," Irene said with neither pleasure nor any indication of understanding. "I see."

The three sat in silence for a moment.

"Josh tells me you were absolutely certain it's the piece my sister painted. The one with two moons and that creature. The griffin with wings."

"Yes. Mrs. Maggiarra"—Keldon caught Josh's glance—"has investigators. I don't know who they are or what she pays them. But they tracked down each of the paintings she wants to acquire. I brought documents with me. They're in the car. It establishes a trail, as best as possible, connecting the man who received the painting to the garage sale where your sister purchased it."

Irene's eyes grew wet. "I hounded her. I was more insistent with her than I was Mother. We were very close as sisters, and I wanted a painting from her. I shouldn't have insisted. She was just as stubborn about it as Mom. Then one day, a painting arrived."

A tear flowed from her.

Josh said, "Irene."

"I'd like to see it, the proof," Irene said amidst a few more tears. "If you don't mind going to your car."

Keldon stood. "Of course. I didn't want to offend you by bringing it into your house. I thought—"

"Please give me a moment. Josh, you too. Go with him to the car. I am very cross with my sister and need a moment to gather myself. We're going to see each other soon, and I plan to yell at her ghost."

Keldon wasn't sure if he should smile at this last small joke, so he kept his face blank and rose from his chair. Josh followed him down the hallway to the front of the house, and Keldon revisited everything with his eyes that made her home seem stylish with that kitschy accent, her whimsy visible in nooks and crannies. He liked this house. And it felt like he was being thrown out. Maybe he would not be asked back inside.

On the front porch, Keldon could not stand the silence.

"Please can we talk about this? Just a little bit?"

"Keldon," Josh said. "I'm sorry. It's too much, man. I loved our dates together—"

"Me too," Keldon said, happy to interrupt before the sentiment was expressed. "And that doesn't happen very often. Or ever. I don't date. I don't have the money to date. I can't afford to rent a car and drive to Madison to see you. I can't afford to take you to dinner until I pay down some of my debt. I'm saying I can't afford this. But I want to try anyway. I don't—"

"I can't, Keldon," Josh said. "I can't get beyond it. And I don't know if it's disgust at the serial-killer part or the fact that you're okay with not knowing why you're doing what you're doing."

"Trust me," Keldon said sadly, "I'm disgusted with myself. Believe it. After Number Four, I pulled over to cry—"

"Keldon," Josh said, pleading. "I don't want to talk about your adventures in art collection. You know what he did to his victims, right? Some of them were kids. I mean, not that it makes it better when it happens to adults—my point is, every time I'm around you, I'm going to be thinking of this and how you don't even know why you're doing it. I can't."

Despite a week's worth of arguments bubbling up inside him, Keldon suddenly felt the futility of trying. All conversational threads, all apologies and explanations led to the tangled knot at the center: a serial killer. Keldon was surprised in facing the end of this beginning relationship that he didn't hate himself more. But it just wasn't possible.

Keldon walked to his rental, sulking, thinking about angry words of retaliation. *Your only friends are people who are dying. You don't decorate your home with personal items because you're so obsessed with death you're afraid of living.* Keldon thought about firing a few angry insights at Josh to see how he liked being judged, but whenever he imagined Josh's face, he saw the earnestness of his hurt and knew that Josh was not trying to be cruel. Keldon melted. He wouldn't say anything mean. He couldn't.

He brought the paperwork to Josh, who nodded at him mournfully. The two men returned to the library where Irene sat waiting, no longer crying nor giving any appearance of having cried. She waited patiently. Quietly. Keldon handed Josh the meager paperwork from Catherine's investigators. Josh gingerly placed her glasses over her eyes and held the papers a comfortable distance so she could read the documents herself.

When she finished, Josh said, "We could call this guy who got the painting and ask him some questions. He's still alive, and his number's on the second page."

"No," Irene said. "I'm sure he's awful but most likely telling the truth. I was always shocked by the piece, actually. Green wasn't Carolyn's favorite color, and I never pictured her as a fantasy landscape painter, so I ignored the probability she didn't paint it herself. I delighted in how whimsical it seemed, given her more serious personality, and whenever I tried to thank her, repeatedly, she always downplayed it, like she was embarrassed to discuss it. This actually makes more sense, that she bought it. She would have to buy something amateurish and terrible so I wouldn't suspect."

Keldon noticed that Mrs. Woullet really seemed like she was dying in this moment. Her face sagged, disappointed. She languished in her wheelchair with none of the bounce she had on their first visit, their secret negotiations when they played him. In this moment, she really seemed sick.

"Your sister had no idea what she had purchased." Keldon looked at his folded hands. "I'm sure she would have never purchased it if she had known. She would have never given it…" He trailed off.

Irene said nothing for a moment.

She said, "You brought sorrow into this house, Mr. Keldon Thurman. It's not your fault my own sister deceived me. But you brought the sad awareness to me, and I'd had quite enough sorrow recently. But it's not your fault. You can have the painting."

Keldon nodded. He hesitated, wondering if he should bring up Mrs. Maggiarra's compensation. But he didn't want to prolong the exchange a second longer. He was crushed by the brief porch conversation with Josh. He wanted to retrieve the painting and leave.

Josh dragged a brown paper bag from between his and Irene's chairs and set it on the small table next to Keldon. Something was wrong. A bag with a small square painting should have flopped to one side, but the bag remained upright and even settled a bit. Although he did not know why the visual was wrong, he understood that he might not see what he expected in the bag.

He opened it and looked inside.

Inside the paper bag was a Ziploc plastic bag of ash.

"We burned it," Irene said. "Josh, send him the video. Please."

Josh nodded at her and avoided Keldon's gaze while picking up his smartphone.

"Keldon, please tell Mrs. Maggiarra what she's doing disgusts me. I won't be part of it. I know this is just a job for you. Josh explained that to me. I hold *her* responsible. I also understand that you're incented based on your retrieval of all fifteen paintings. I am very sorry for the inconvenience this may cause you. I understand you won't get paid now, not the full amount. But I could not sell her the painting for any price."

"It's sent," Josh said quietly.

He set the phone next to Irene and put his face in his hands.

"My phone is in the car," Keldon said, still reeling from the surprise of the burned painting. "I didn't bring it inside so we wouldn't be interrupted."

Irene said, "I insisted Josh film us burning the painting in a trash can because I wanted your Mrs. Maggiarra to understand Merrick's art was truly destroyed. I did not want her suspicion that perhaps I had decided to search for a better offer. Josh doused it in gasoline first, but you can definitely tell it's the painting you desired. The video is quite long, maybe four or five minutes of the painting burning into nothing. These are the ashes. If it helps your case, tell Mrs. Maggiarra you succeeded in your quest and collected Number Five. And if it doesn't help you, I'm sorry. Some things are more important than money."

Keldon stared at the ashes and panicked. He could never earn the bonus that would give him a second chance at college or something, *something* to get out of temp work and retail jobs. Those dreams were over, burnt to ash. He had already failed to collect all fifteen paintings.

He felt an almost sick relief that he would most likely be fired. Mrs. Maggiarra would have to fire him. How could she not, given this colossal failure?

"I think you should go," Irene said.

Keldon stood.

Josh stood and looked at the floor.

"I'm sorry for all of this," Keldon said, unsure if he apologized to Irene or Josh. "I'm sorry to bring sorrow into your home. Both of your homes."

He did not wait for a reply, fearing there would be none, and as no one tried to stop him on the way from the library, his assumption was proven correct. He walked to the front door with the bag of ash. Carrying it, he could see they had left one corner burned but not completely destroyed. He wondered if that was intentional or they felt the 97% cremation was sufficient. What did it matter? The painting was destroyed along with his hope for a different life.

The familiar sensation of financial dread overtook him, a phantom that had drifted away since his recent employment. But it never drifted too far. Now it returned and chided him for not stocking up on cheap macaroni and cheese.

When he reached the car, he checked to see his new message, and sure enough, he had received a large video file that took an extra few minutes to download. He watched it in his car, the flames licking James Wayne Merrick's painting, a grotesque and failed attempt to create something beautiful now reduced to cold ash in the trunk of the rental.

Chapter Nine

Because Catherine wasn't expecting news, he did not call and update her. He wanted to decide how to address this. He wanted to figure out his finances since presenting the bag of ash certainly meant his termination. After twenty-four hours, he realized he could not delay any longer and scheduled an appointment to see her.

He took the bag of ash, his cell phone with the video, and drove to Glen Ellyn later that day. Keldon grimly accepted his fate. He didn't care. He had already been fired from a more important job—Josh's new boyfriend.

* * * *

Catherine watched the video holding Keldon's phone, occasionally glancing at the Ziploc bag of ash sitting on her desk.

"Destroyed," Keldon said in a voice he felt was triumphant but a little subdued so as to not gloat. He was aware saying the word was completely unnecessary, yet he couldn't help but say it, an exclamation point to the video and bag of ash. He couldn't gloat as he would soon be fired. He had to live through the humiliation. Maybe she would pay his final expense check if he was subservient. Maybe a little severance pay. It always came down to money.

Catherine watched the video a second time before handing the phone back to Keldon. "Send me this video."

Keldon was disappointed in her reaction. He wanted something, her face turning red, her gasping in shock and rage at one of her precious art pieces destroyed. But she expressed nothing, nothing that would satisfy his confused desire. No spark of humanity, disappointment, or frustration. As he texted the raw footage to her, he hated her a little bit. Keldon was disgusted with himself for ending up with people who did not feel, could not express themselves. Why was he drawn to cold people, like Steven and Aamir?

Well, except Joshua. Josh unlocked feelings in him. Josh shared feelings with him. He remembered Josh's confession standing at the tomato bed and how he asked Keldon not to reveal he was acting or playing along. How much the date mattered to him. The feelings caught in Keldon's throat, and he suppressed them. He had to.

Catherine examined the corner of the painting that had not been burned, studied it through the plastic, and when she was finished, she returned the plastic back to the paper bag Irene had given Keldon. She set the bag behind her as she had every other acquired painting. Keldon took a deep breath to prepare for his doom.

"We need to discuss Acquisition Number Seven," Catherine said. "I don't like this idea of bidding against someone else who wants the painting. I want to hear every word they said. I may have my investigators poke around to see if they can uncover who else is bidding."

Keldon couldn't believe his ears.

Catherine opened her file for Number Seven and pulled her glasses up around her neck. "I need to know exactly—"

"I quit," Keldon said.

The words hung in the room between them, surprising them both.

Catherine said nothing but turned her head slightly as if she had misunderstood.

Keldon hadn't realized what he wanted until he heard himself say it aloud, to be free of this monstrous task. But if she wasn't going to fire him, he would have to free himself.

"You're a ghoul," Keldon said, his voice shaking. "James Merrick was a sick, twisted, horrible person. And you're paying thousands of dollars for his art. I hate being involved with this horrible job. I hate who I am when I'm negotiating with people for your filthy acquisitions. I hate myself."

Keldon realized with great sadness that this was true, that he hated himself and his obsession with money. He commanded himself not to cry, but as soon as the word *cry* danced in his brain, fat tears rolled down his face.

Catherine Maggiarra said nothing, but her features softened, and he hated her even more for her pity.

"This is disgusting," he said and wiped tears away angrily. "You shouldn't be celebrating serial-killer art. Nobody should. You're a monster, Mrs. Maggiarra. I don't care why you're collecting this art. It's horrible."

Keldon gave himself a moment to collect his emotions, to stop shaking. To stop the tears. But they did not stop. He did not dissolve into an uncontrollable crying jag, but his tears popped out nevertheless, too many to pretend an allergy or speck of dust.

With a shaking voice, he said, "I think you should pay me for my latest expenses and last week's work. I'm not asking for the big bonus because obviously I failed to get all fifteen paintings. And I'm sorry I failed. But I'm going to ask you to pay that final expense check for the rental car, even though I screwed up and only have this bag of ash to show you. I just think it's fair."

He found himself wiping his eyes again and again. He couldn't even see her, couldn't meet her gaze. But gradually, the tears stopped coming. Keldon realized calling her a *ghoul* was probably not the best tactic to entice her to pay him for services rendered. But somehow, it thrilled him, even now, that he dared to speak authentically, even if it meant losing the money. His stomach lurched when he thought about his lack of prospects. Nine months ago, he had crafted a list of things he must sell and the sequence in which he would sell them, saving favorites, such as suits and his heavy leather jacket as the absolute last items on his list. After today, the suits would go next. And then he had nothing. But he could stop hating himself, which was something.

Now that he was beyond tears, he dared look into her eyes, finding her familiar curiosity, as if she found him to be puzzling.

"No," Catherine said.

Keldon nodded. Mrs. Maggiarra did not seem like the kind of businesswoman to pay out a half-finished job, so he wasn't surprised. He found himself eager to be rid of her, this house, the mistake of taking the role of serial-killer-art acquisition expert. He needed to be gone.

He stood up.

Catherine said, "Please sit. What I meant was that I do not accept your resignation."

Keldon didn't understand her words.

He said, "I quit."

"No," she said, "you do not. You're more perfect for this job than ever. I do not release you from service. You signed a contract. I ask you to sit."

Keldon remained standing, uncertain. He had just called her a ghoul. And a monster. How could she not accept his resignation?

"*Please*," Catherine said.

He looked at her and saw something he had not seen in her before, a vulnerability. She did not seem close to crying or breaking down, but a softening was present. She really wanted him to sit, but she understood it was within his power to leave.

Keldon lowered himself into his chair gingerly, confused and wary.

"I want to tell you a story about my husband," Catherine said. "And if you still wish to quit, I will honor your resignation and pay you for the wonderful service you provided. But I am hoping you will stay and continue to assist me."

Keldon nodded, though he knew there was nothing she could say to convince him. But he would humor her.

"My husband"—her customary sharpness returned—"was a fool. A court jester. He could make anyone laugh, put anyone at ease. When we attended parties, children would flock to him because he would pull quarters from behind their ears and make them giggle. Men sought his counsel on serious matters because it was understood that behind his silliness was a quiet, reflective soul. He was not overly attractive, not Hollywood-model attractive, but women threw themselves at him constantly because after five minutes around him, you loved yourself more. You felt funny and smart. He shifted from hilarity to soft sadness exactly as the moment demanded him. Everyone adored him."

Mrs. Maggiarra glanced out the window. "No one adored him more than I did."

Her sharp gaze returned to Keldon, and he was surprised by the borderline anger in her eyes. It did not seem to match her heartfelt words.

She said, "He loved me. He loved *me*. I am a sharp, angular woman. I am Mensa-level smart, and I ran my Human Resources division with a professionalism that was benchmarked and studied by Fortune 100 companies. I was twice profiled in professional Human Resources literature and once in the *Wall Street Journal*. And that ridiculous fool loved *me*. He made me laugh. He softened my sharpness and made me likeable to others. With him I had friends. I found myself laughing at parties instead of complaining at the idiot small talk all around me. His love was the best thing in my life. No contest. We were married for forty-three years."

She paused.

Keldon found himself surprised at the strong emotion behind her confession and yet taken aback at the almost-hostility in her expression, in her eyes.

"We never had children. We never *wanted* children. Well-meaning friends would wistfully explain what perfect parents we would make, how lucky our children would be, and we smiled and accepted their compliments with grace. We definitely loved children. Perhaps ours was a selfish marriage because we were content with each other and the children brought into our lives through friends and family."

"His name was Galten," Catherine said, and at last her tone shifted into something softer.

"When he retired, he began teaching piano lessons. Not to just anyone, only neighborhood children whose parents we knew or children he liked. He did not care for developing virtuosos or molding the next perfect concertmaster. He just liked watching children struggle and then find success. He had patience for listening to wrong note after wrong note. He could inspire a child to find something within themselves. We had a routine. When the piano lesson was over, the child would sit with me in the kitchen and talk to me about school until their parents arrived. I would have warm cookies waiting after the lesson."

She smiled, and her eyes grew wet. "Me. *Baking cookies.* Listening to children babble about reading and teachers they loved and what my husband said to them. I would compliment them on their playing and tell them my favorite parts of their song. Byron Mercer would have laughed his ass off if he could see me playing the role of Mrs. Claus to Galten's jolly Santa. I loved it. I loved my life with Galten."

Keldon felt himself growing softer toward Catherine, though he had no clue how this tale involved him or serial-killer art. He already regretted calling her a ghoul.

"Hector Chantalo was one of Galten's favorite students. He was black-haired Mexican boy with one brown eye and one blue. There's a word for that, I knew it at one time. Hector confessed to my husband how the kids at school teased him, how they insisted it meant he had two different fathers, one with brown eyes and one father with blue. He cried on that piano bench, and when I heard the tears, I came from the kitchen to find Galten with his arm around Hector's shoulders inventing a story, a wonderful and silly story about a king from a faraway land, a king gifted with two different eye colors. Galten always invented stories for children, for me. Galten winked at me, and I backed away. When Hector came into the kitchen after his lesson, he happily repeated the story and asked if it were true. I told him 'Absolutely.' I even added to it, because that's what my husband could do. Make you play along. I am not a soft woman. My whole married life I danced to his beautiful lunacy and I loved it."

She stopped speaking.

Keldon watched her, saw her trembling lip, and then looked away, glanced around the solemn office with its muted maroon and oak décor, giving her a moment to compose herself.

Her voice returned to her customary steel when she spoke. "Hector Chantalo was James Wayne Merrick's seventeenth victim. Nobody knew that, of course, when he first disappeared. The weekend Hector went missing, I skipped our annual shareholder meeting to help our neighborhood patrol search. Skipping that meeting was a great offense to the shareholders. Byron Mercer almost fired me over the phone. But I knew my priorities. Galten adored that child, and he needed me. Hector needed me. We did everything we could in those first two weeks. We searched. We contributed reward money. We hung up flyers and took food to Mrs. Chantalo. After a week or two missing, it was generally assumed the boy's errant father had kidnapped his son, perhaps taken him back to Mexico. Galten was saddened, damaged by the disappearance, but Galten had endured disappointments— the death of his brother, both parents, a best friend with cancer. Galten had endured hardships and managed to keep himself the same, goofy, loveable man. Saddened by life's sorrows, yes, yet he still managed to find quarters behind children's ears."

Catherine presented herself as she always had to Keldon, all business.

"It killed Galten when they found Hector's body in that monster's house. The news programs delighted in reporting horrific details of what the victims endured and how they met their ends. Nobody could escape the details and updates for months. Over and over, newspapers and television explained how many stab wounds had been inflicted or how some had been repeatedly strangled to unconsciousness and then revived only to be strangled again, how victims were kept alive for weeks sometimes."

"Stop." Keldon found himself shaking. "I don't want to hear this."

"Nobody does." Catherine stood and walked away from him. "We certainly didn't. But you couldn't escape it. Everyone talked about it for three months. Hector was only Victim Seventeen to most of the world. They had no idea how hard he practiced for his piano lessons. After Hector's death, Galten never found any more quarters behind children's ears."

Keldon said nothing but hung his head.

"Newspapers and television don't tell you," she said, "about what a horror like this does to the community. They interview the parents, stick fat microphones in their faces and say, 'How does it feel?' Or they get the shot of the parent sobbing and that's the end. Cut. Play the footage. But evil like James Wayne Merrick also destroys the fabric of the community, of everyone touched by that poison. Children learned to live in fear that true monsters walk among us. Parents screamed at their kids who dared to ride their bikes around the block out of eyesight. Neighbors watched each other with greater suspicion. Merrick stole my husband's joy. It was murdered with the death of a little king bearing one brown eye and one blue."

Catherine Maggiarra turned to face Keldon. From across the room, he heard the cold fury in her voice. "I like your phrase *filthy acquisitions* because that's what happened to Galten. When Merrick's murders exploded into the public eye, Galten acquired some of the filth, the poison. You go through life, and disappointments come your way. Death. Dreams that never come true. You acquire a little filth. You lose a little of your dreams. You get obsessed with money or status, or a raise. Filthy acquisitions. But not Galten. None of that ever weighed him down. He did the impossible, survived for almost seventy-four years with his joy intact. That is, until Merrick murdered my husband. When Galten died two years later, he was no longer the same man."

She returned to her desk and sat down.

In her professional voice, she said, "It sickens me that Merrick's art is in the world. That people want to sell it, make money on it, show it off to their friends as a curiosity. 'Look at this. A real serial killer painted it.' Disgusting. I cannot erase Merrick from the world, but I can make goddamn sure his art career is over. I will pay anything for those paintings. *Anything.* But I prefer not to pay much at all because it disgusts me people like the Turners profit off a man who killed Hector and Galten. I hate it. At least Irene Woullet had no idea what she possessed. And once she found out, she destroyed it. I'm sending her the money anyway. She's a hero to me."

Keldon now understood. "You don't mind that she burned that painting because you're going to destroythese paintings yourself."

"Absolutely," Catherine said with an angry vigor Keldon had only glimpsed in the past. But now the fire was revealed. "Once I've collected all that remain, I will rent a warehouse or someplace private and invite relatives of the victims to come. We will mourn together. No camera crew. No videos. We will create a pile of these paintings, a bonfire. Families of victims will speak of their loved ones if they wish, and together we will burn this evil man's shitty art until nothing remains but ash. This will not bring back their sons and daughters, their girlfriends or cousins. But mourning, I've discovered, is something you engage in for the rest of your life. This might be a healing milestone for a wound that will never heal."

Keldon felt a greater sadness, a sadness from a deeper place beyond his own self-loathing. He wasn't sure what to say. Eventually, he said, "I would have liked to meet your husband."

Catherine nodded.

She said, "A year ago, I inherited money from a rich cousin. A second cousin. Nobody knew she was wealthy or how she acquired it. I had only met her twice. I gave her financial advice once, stock tips during a family reunion, but that was the extent of our relationship. Obviously, I wouldn't call us close. But her money came to me. Apparently, she had no one else. Galten and I were well off from our respective careers. Not rich, but comfortable. I don't want to go on widow vacations or visit expensive salons. I'd rather plant flowers in my yard and go to Chicago for the Fourth of July fireworks with Galten. And since he's dead, well, I'll just stay home."

"So you decided to buy these paintings."

"Whatever the cost," Catherine said. "I will have them. And it must be done legally because I plan to destroy them. I can't have someone sue me for custody of a painting I no longer possess. Everything must remain above legal reproach."

Keldon said, "And Mr. Mercer?"

"He is my friend of many years and knows everything. He has no problem with my throwing around his name in these filthy acquisitions. Over the years, he saw me with Galten at company parties and one or two summer picnics. He witnessed Galten and I bungle karaoke, and then he understood Galten's unique gift to my life."

Keldon looked down, feeling worse for calling her a ghoul. He felt he couldn't do anything right.

He asked, "But why all the secrecy? Why wouldn't you just tell me all of this?"

Catherine fiddled with the pens on her desk, aligning them in rows. After a moment, she spoke. "Before hiring you I tried to make the first acquisition myself. I showed up unannounced at the home. Explained my intention. Offered them money. When they found I intended to destroy the painting, they refused to sell it. Demanded I leave. Honestly, it hadn't dawned on me someone might refuse to sell to me because I planned to destroy the art. It's ugly art, and Merrick was a horror who delighted in ending lives before they were even fully begun. I hadn't dreamed—"

She stopped.

Looking straight at him, she said, "Part of it was my demeanor, I know. I was a bull in a china shop, waving around a check demanding, 'Give me the damn painting.' I am not graceful. Subtle. After they refused to sell to me and kicked me out, I realized I needed to hire someone to make the actual acquisition. And if that person had no idea what I was going to do with the art, they couldn't lie or wouldn't have to lie when making the purchase. Your face can't give anything away if you have no inkling of my true motives."

Keldon reeled from the explanations, the reasons. He stared at her in wonder, this curious combination of hard and soft in her. He had no clue as to its existence, this softer side.

After a moment of silence, he felt someone should speak. "What happened to those people who refused to sell?"

"They're still on the list. They're Acquisition Number Fifteen. I was hoping a little time and your deft touch would persuade them to come around."

He did not nod. He didn't know what to say. The sadness he felt in hearing her story, her connection to Merrick, was tempered with frustration. If he had known why Catherine was collecting the serial-killer art, he could have told Josh. He could have salvaged the date. Josh would approve of his job now, he felt sure of that. He felt a shortness rising, a confused anger.

"I wish you would have told me. It would have made things easier with Josh. I could have explained myself. Why couldn't you tell *me*, even if you didn't want the sellers to know?"

"Keldon, you were an unknown quantity. Perhaps perfect for this job, but I didn't trust you. I couldn't risk you accidentally revealing my intentions. Perhaps my years of running a Human Resources division played a role. I do not share information that does not need to be shared."

He looked down, feeling sad by the whole revelation, including the fact that he was untrustworthy.

Catherine said, "I hired you for all the reasons I explained. I required someone tenacious about acquiring the paintings. Your distinguished looks and somewhat aristocratic bearing would help negotiate lower prices, I felt sure of that. That was all true. But your outburst a few moments ago and your threatening to quit showed me another side of you. I'm delighted this work disgusts you. I know your financial situation. It couldn't have been easy to give up life-changing money to call me a *ghoul*. I find myself having faith in people again. First, Irene Woullet burns the painting rather than let me do god knows what with it. And then, you, Keldon. If a young man like you would turn down six-figure riches and admit he hated himself for this work…"

Catherine clamped her mouth shut. Keldon looked down. They avoided each other for several long seconds.

"I don't want you to quit," she said, her voice husky. "You're even more perfect for this role than before because now I know your heart and you're a good man."

Keldon felt his head get warm as if the tears might return so he did not look at her.

"Please help me," Catherine said. "Please continue acquiring the art. I can't do this alone. If Galten were here, I could be more entertaining and come across nicer. I would bake you cookies or something. I know I'm stern. I always have been."

Keldon looked up into her eyes and allowed her to see a fat tear roll down his cheek. Catherine's expression remained unchanged, but her face mirrored his in one regard, a single tear escaping her as well. They watched each other in silence, neither making a move to wipe away the evidence of grief, silently creating a new pact between them.

Chapter Ten

Keldon waited a full day before driving to Madison.

He spent hour after hour debating the trip, arguing Josh's perspective that Catherine's revelations meant nothing, this news that the paintings would be destroyed did not matter because Keldon had still accepted the job not knowing this outcome. Wasn't Keldon the same person regardless of Catherine's intentions? But to Keldon it mattered. He had tried to quit. He had called Catherine a ghoul. It had made a good impression on Catherine, so perhaps it would positively influence Josh.

He had to try.

Catherine was less than enthusiastic when Keldon explained he wished to tell Josh the paintings' ultimate fate. He needed to tell Josh that he had quit. That he had scorned the money and tried to walk away.

"I have feelings for him," Keldon said. "Strong ones."

When she saw Keldon's eyes, brimming with new tears, she closed her mouth.

Catherine had a hard time refusing.

And as long as she was in a giving mood, Keldon asked for a little cash advance. "Dating money," he called it when explaining the sum to her.

But before he confronted Josh, he wanted to be more ready. He had underestimated Josh's reaction to the original Merrick revelation, and he refused to do so again. He wanted to be ready to see Josh. Keldon needed to steel himself for more potential rejection.

He drove the entire way considering opening lines, begging for five minutes, asking Josh to please consider taking the chance. Keldon wanted this. He wanted to learn more about beekeeping and vegetable farming. He wanted to go to the farmers' market three weeks in a row and not complain. And he didn't want to do it to *please* Josh. He wanted it for himself.

As he passed the signs for Madison, Keldon found himself thinking of the capitol, though he was nowhere near it. He wanted to see the white-frosted dome with its cake topper. Instead, he drove straight to Josh's neighborhood, his memories lapsing into the luncheon bike ride to the Thai pavilion.

He knocked several times before questioning whether Josh was even home. He had no idea of Josh's work schedule, so he could be at any number of client homes, he supposed. Or out getting groceries. Keldon wasn't sure what to do. He walked to the backyard nervously, not eager to interrupt some solitary task or frighten Josh, but unwilling to accept defeat because no one answered the front door. Josh was not in back. The tomato plants in their jointly constructed bed thrived, were taller by a few inches since Keldon saw them last. He was proud of that, though he had done nothing but move dirt and arrange wood. The border of marigolds appeared to be doing their job as the leaves appeared unmolested. He smiled when he saw the vines surging upward, remembering how a little piece of him was forever in this junky back yard.

After waiting on the front steps for another half-hour, he drove to Irene Woullet's home.

Keldon had mixed feelings about seeing her. He wanted to explain Catherine's intentions and explain how Mrs. Maggiarra would still like to offer compensation and her sincere thanks. But he also remembered how ashamed he had felt after their last visit and so he would reluctantly face her, which would undoubtedly summon that awful gut feeling again, the disgust with himself. Josh would be there, likely, and that made him nervous as well, attempting to explain to both wronged parties at the same time. He had hoped to catch them apart.

He pulled up to the Woullet house and was surprised to see a taller man with a ring of black hair headed inside. It was no one he recognized. A woman emerged from the front door and after exchanging a word with the man on the front walk, continued toward the street, toward Keldon, though he understood almost immediately she wasn't coming to see him. She clicked a remote and the taillights flickered for a car parked in front of Irene's house. He wondered briefly about the unusual activity, but also considered that he had no idea of Irene Woullet's daily routines. These could be doctors. Other nurses. Relatives.

Keldon left his car to approach her. "Excuse me, can you tell me if Mrs. Woullet is home today?"

The woman stopped her slow walk to the car and regarded Keldon carefully. "Are you from the nursing agency?"

Keldon said, "No."

"Hospice?"

"No. I'm a friend. Well, an acquaintance."

"What's your name," the woman said.

"Keldon Thurman," he said politely and offered his hand.

Keldon took an extra moment to study this woman in front of him, a collection of hard facial planes and short grayish-blonde hair. The haircut did not soften her face, and he was surprised to see something like suspicion in her eyes.

"My mother never mentioned you," she said.

Keldon said, "You have me at a disadvantage because I'm afraid I don't know you."

"I'm Darlene Woullet. Irene's daughter. How did you know my mother, again?"

"I only met her a few times. I have some news for her."

Darlene Woullet eyed him with suspicion. "She died last night. How did you know her?"

"Oh," Keldon said, surprised. He looked at the house, expecting to see Irene in the front window, sitting in her chair, confirming her daughter's report. "I'm so sorry." He looked at Darlene. "I really am. I only met her three times, but she seemed very nice."

Darlene pried for more details, and Keldon gave the rough outline, explaining he had been tasked with acquiring a piece of art from Irene Woullet but the deal had fallen through. Darlene asked additional questions, and while Keldon understood she had a right to know everything about her mother's estate, he found himself reluctant to provide information. He wanted to leave. He needed to find Josh immediately.

"May I ask if the day nurse is here, Joshua Greene?"

"He was here earlier," Irene's daughter said. "He picked up a few things of his and a muffin pan I'm not entirely convinced that pan wasn't my mom's, and he left. He hasn't been here for hours."

Keldon digested this. Josh wasn't at home. Wasn't here.

"I'm very sorry about your mother," Keldon said. "I have to call my employer. Will you excuse me?"

Darlene Woullet nodded, but her face betrayed her mistrust.

Keldon stepped away and pretended to make the call. In truth, he didn't want more conversation with Irene's daughter, who seemed intent on understanding the exact nature of the art acquisition. It didn't matter, not to Keldon. He needed to find Josh.

He faked a phone conversation all the way back to the car, watching the tall man leave the house once again and return to his vehicle. Keldon didn't know whether he was from the funeral home, the nursing agency, or something else. He didn't care. He had to find Josh immediately.

After another minute of fake conversation, he started his rental car and eased back onto the street, pretending not to see Darlene Woullet walk faster toward him and raise her hand in protest.

He could not think of where Josh might be. Of course Josh probably had dozens of spots where he might go to be alone, favorite bars, a favorite park. Keldon briefly considered the Thai pavilion and decided to add it to the list of unlikely, but still possible, locations. He drove to Josh's house to double-check and found nothing changed.

There was one place that Keldon thought possible. One place.

* * * *

Keldon parked his car a block away from the Wisconsin state capitol. The capitol's dome impressed him the way it did previously, majestic, ethereal frosting. He took little pleasure in the wedding cake comparison today. If Josh wasn't here, he didn't know where to go next. Perhaps the Thai pavilion.

His eyes jerked to the sea of tulips as soon as they came into view, and he completely forgot his immediate, pressing business. They were uniform in their direction, hundreds upon hundreds of them, vibrating colors off their very stems, demanding attention be paid. He marveled at their numbers and was pleased to see the yellow-and-orange-streaked tulips also shared space with bloodred ones, a few white ones, and a separate field of lavender and white tulips, as if diversity were valued here, more so than attractive conformity. He understood how people would make a point to visit this, to stare at this. It was beauty worth ogling. He walked and stared at them, mesmerized by their numbers.

He walked along the side of the capitol, now aware of how many others stared with him, some taking photos trying to capture the tulips' vastness and their sprawl across the capitol lawn. The pictures would fail to capture the surprised strength of this many united flowers. But the photos would be pretty, nonetheless. Keldon came upon them, closer and closer, and recognized the shape of a man sitting directly in them, possibly sitting on one of them, defiantly protesting their presence.

Josh.

Josh looked in almost every direction during the long minute it took Keldon to reach him, every direction except at Keldon. Keldon wasn't sure how to approach him, whether Josh wanted to be alone, how he would react to his conversation with Catherine and his continuing to work under her employ. He didn't even know if they would speak of that today. Josh had just lost one of his best friends, possibly his only friend. Keldon stood on the sidewalk and waited until Josh's attention inevitably wandered in his direction.

"Oh," Josh said with surprise when he finally noticed.

Keldon didn't say anything, suddenly not ready to speak. Josh looked beleaguered, a word without very many applications, but here, Keldon felt the word fit. Josh seemed exhausted and worn, another grief added to his life, another filthy acquisition to steal his joy.

Josh's confusion melted, and a tear stumbled down his cheek. "How did you get here? Why are you here?"

"I came to see you," Keldon said. "I wanted to talk to you about something. But then I got to Irene's house and I found out, you know…"

"Yeah." Josh's face creased in hurt as if he had just heard the news. "She died."

"How?"

"They don't know. Maybe an aneurism. The night nurse gave her the right dosage of medication so it wasn't drug-related, they don't think. They don't know for sure."

"I'm sorry," Keldon said.

The two men didn't say anything for a moment. Keldon watched and worried, unsure how to proceed. Keldon didn't know how to date someone. He was not used to abandoning his role as the pleaser.

Josh lifted a book in his right hand and said, "Did she call you?"

"Who?"

"Irene. She told you to come today?"

"Irene? No. No, I had absolutely no idea about her until I got here and started looking for you. I came because I wanted to see you. I wanted to see you again. I miss you."

This made Josh crinkle his face and cry in earnest, putting his hand to his face.

Keldon did not understand what was happening, but recognized its significance, so he navigated through the tulips and positioned himself behind Josh. Because of how closely planted the tulips were, he could not sit easily without snapping a flower off at the base, so he knelt to one side behind Josh and wrapped his arms around him. Josh cried a little, cried harder, and stopped suddenly, wiping his arm across his face.

"I'm not as good with death as I thought," Josh said. "I'm a hypocrite."

"You're not a hypocrite."

"Trust me, I am," he said sadly. "Here I am telling you how natural death is, how easy it is, why fear it, and I can't believe what happened. She's gone. She was one of my few friends in Madison. I wasn't ready for this."

Keldon put his head against Josh's back and resisted the urge to rock him back and forth. Gentle rocking didn't feel right, but he wanted to do *something* to be of more comfort.

Josh continued. "Four days ago, she reminded me that when she died she wanted me to take her favorite book, *Great Expectations*. Two days ago, she pointed at the table where she kept it and said that she wanted me to take it right away, before her daughter could inventory the library books. It was a gift she wanted me to have *right away*. She made me promise to get the book."

Keldon noticed the hardbound copy of *Great Expectations* in Josh's hands.

"She left me a note inside," Josh said and pulled the bookmark from the pages. "Read it. You're mentioned."

Heart-pounding anxiety raced through Keldon instantly, as if he had been caught doing something wrong. Why was he named?

He didn't have to wait long for the answer as Josh unfolded the letter and, over Josh's shoulder, Keldon read the note from Irene Woullet in her exaggerated script.

Joshua, my dear—and I do not use this word lightly—friend,

I'm having a good day today. Look at my handwriting. It's big and loopy, but I haven't written this well without trembling in weeks or maybe months. I forgot the pleasure of a handwritten note. I have forgotten many pleasures except for a handful, including your company and the treats you bake. I do love your lemon scones with blueberry crème.

When we hosted dinner parties, my husband Martin stood in the doorway, waving goodnight to our guests. Not me. I don't do lingering good-byes. So allow me to be brief.

Thank you for the great care. You're a damn good nurse. I felt safe and confident in your company as a professional, more so than with other caregivers. Certainly more than with Marlene. I've already talked to her, Josh, but that's not why I'm writing. I'm writing because you were an even better friend to me. I loved our time laughing and talking about books. You need to read those book titles I gave you. And even better than the books, I found a confidant in you, someone to tell things I have always wanted to say aloud.

I have one more thing to say aloud.

Give Keldon another chance. I swear it won't make me any happier in the afterlife for you to date him. I know we both find his day job repugnant. But darling, remember that you worked a job you hated for a long time until your schooling was almost entirely paid off. We all do things we don't want to, and we do it for money.

Don't wait until you're dying to recognize what's important. Forgive him.

Did you like how I slipped in that comment about the afterlife? Given our conversations on the subject, I thought you might appreciate that. I die not knowing what to think about what comes next. I might be an angel, a ghost, or cease to exist. I don't know. I guess I'll find out.

With all my heart for your friendship and love,

Irene

P.S. One more thing. Your blond brownies are a little dry. Think maybe about adding more condensed milk or maybe some cranberries or a chewy fruit to them. Craisins, maybe.

P.P.S. I lied. Your blond brownies are perfect. I just added that first P.S. because I didn't want to stop writing this letter. I've told you what you mean to me, so you know that already, right? Good. So I'll just say this. I love you.

Josh cried again when he finished reading it, and Keldon held him tighter, trying not to cry himself. A few curious picture-takers frowned in their direction as they ruined a clear shot of the state capitol's fields of stunning yellow and orange tulips. Keldon blinked and stared them down as a way of steeling himself to be strong.

After a minute, Josh stopped and wiped his face again. In a weak voice, he said, "She didn't send you? She didn't call?"

"No," Keldon said, the word shaking as it came out of him. He realized he might cry a little despite his attempts to hold it in.

Josh said in a desolate voice, "Why did you come?"

"To see you. To talk."

Josh said, "About what?"

Keldon said, "It can wait. We have time."

Josh seemed to relax upon hearing this. "Okay."

Keldon thought to himself, *We have time.*

In a shaky voice, Josh said, "Please don't leave."

Keldon squeezed tighter until he felt he could speak without crying. "I'm not going anywhere. I'm with you."

The two men sat in the field of tulips in front of the Wisconsin state capitol, feeling sad and feeling hopeful.

The End

Trademark Acknowledgement

Edmond Manning

EDMOND MANNING has always been fascinated by fiction: how ordinary words could be sculpted into heartfelt emotions, how heartfelt emotions could leave an imprint inside you stronger than the real world. Mr. Manning never felt worthy to seek publication until recently, when he accidentally stumbled into his own writer's voice that fit perfectly, like his favorite skull-print, fuzzy jammies. He finally realized that he didn't have to write like Charles Dickens or Armistead Maupin, two author heroes, and that perhaps his own fiction was juuuuuuust right, because it was his true voice, so he looked around the scrappy word kingdom that he created for himself and shouted, "I'M HOME!" He is now a writer.

In addition to fiction, Edmond enjoys writing nonfiction on his blog, http://www.edmondmanning.com. When not writing, he can be found either picking raspberries in the back yard or eating panang curry in an overstuffed chair upstairs, reading comic books.

Feel free to contact him at remembertheking@comcast.net.

Also by
Edmond Manning

King Perry
King Mai
I Probably Shouldn't Have Done That

CPSIA information can be obtained at www.ICGtesting.com
Printed in the USA
BVOW04s1023140415

396068BV00001B/5/P